Breaking the Mating Bond

Wiccan Haus Book 17

By
Dominique Eastwick

Copyright © 2016 by Dominique Eastwick
ISBN: 978-1-68361-082-3
Cover art by Fiona Jayde

Published by Decadent Publishing Company, LLC
Look for us online at:
www.decadentpublishing.com

Dedication

Dedicated to my Wiccan Haus sisters who continue to inspire me with how they see the island.

Chapter One

"So there is a way to break the bond?" Janessa Rowan unbraided her hair for the umpteenth time since she had entered the office of her friend and mentor an hour ago.

"Few magics, light or dark, are unbreakable with the knowledge and the tools, as you, a curse breaker, know." Allias Lindinbeck kept his nose in the book inches from his face. Even with spectacles an inch thick, the man could not see past the nose on his own face, but she loved him and prayed he had the information she needed.

"I have both at least in the way of contacts." Janessa Rowan watched the hustle of the main city from the window bench. Ever since the murder of her family years earlier, she no longer lived in the mortal world, hoping the safety of the para world would give her a degree of safety. It was at least a hope of hers.

After a few minutes of hums and humphs, Allias bumped the pile of books beside him, causing them to crash to the floor. Janessa stood, picked up the books, and restacked them, ensuring they lay in the order from before the fall. To someone who didn't know Professor Lindinbeck, the office would appear a hoarder's wonderland. But there was a method to his messiness, and, in it, he knew where every book lay. Having been his private assistant for years, she could replace them in their pattern.

Over the rim of his glasses, Allias cast a glance at her. She knew he didn't see her, but the professor in him could still make his students rethink everything they knew. "Are you sure? Once you do this, there may be no turning back."

Nodding, she ran her fingers over the jewel-encrusted dagger she had placed on one of the side tables when she arrived. Her husband's heirloom, the Knife of Moshchnost, the symbol of his people. Mythos supposed it gave the Božović power to rule their people and yet none of his line had been able to touch it in a hundred years. Although Allias referred to the issues with her bond mate, she had so much more to deal with before the full moon rose again. "It's the right thing to do."

The old wizard didn't argue. She knew he wouldn't. This was the right thing for everyone involved. If all went as planned, the three persons hurting would become only one and a serious wrong would be righted. "I only worry it is a great burden to add to your shoulders in a week promising to be draining on all the Rowans."

"Do you think it's too much on them?"

He shrugged. "Who is to say what is too much for a Rowan? I include you in the statement. The family is resilient and strong, and I think they will only get stronger after the coven meeting. Healing can bring great strength. And your powers will be at their strongest on the night when Luna is at her fullest."

They all needed healing, none more so than her cousin Cyrus who still carried great guilt over the events of a night nearly seven years ago. Assassins following him for months, yet under the protection of Rekkus Duteigr no one had managed to get close. They wanted Cyrus and, in order to hurt him, settled with killing those he loved. At the next full moon on Beltane, the surviving Rowan cousins would help those killed find peace and move to the next life and those left behind move on as best they could.

"If you are determined to break the bond, you must meet all three requirements. The person breaking it must be pure of heart. The reason must be selfless in nature, and your love for him must be true."

She didn't answer, but she didn't think Allias expected an answer. "You must chant the spell and say aloud three times, I release you. The final time must be before the rising sun following Beltane." He wrote down what she needed for the spell, the exact directions, and, finally, what to expect with the spell complete. "This doesn't give you much time."

"It's all set up. The family is heading to the Wiccan Haus for the memorial for our sisters lost seven years ago. As you know, being bonded, my husband cannot go more than a few days from my side, and I have convinced him to bring his father who has some ailments my cousins can assist with."

"So you shall work on the Knife of Moshchnost while you are there?"

"I believe Sarka has the keys to unlocking this curse. She has the books I need in her private library."

He nodded his agreement. "And Narsaria?"

Janessa tried not to flinch at her stepsister's name. It was she, after all, to whom her husband's heart belonged. "Though not part of the coven, she is family and invited to the island to observe the memorial."

"I have never trusted her." Allias rubbed the bridge of his nose before placing the glasses on the stack of books beside him. He appeared frail and tired, closing his eyes and leaning his head back against the side of the old leather Chesterfield chair.

"Beauty as striking as Narsaria's can breed distrust. Besides, it's hard to fault her. Narsaria and Silvano were a couple long before I came along." Even saying their names in the same sentence hurt.

Extending his long bony finger in her direction, he mumbled, "But the Fates chose you, not her, as his bondmate."

"The Fates could not have guessed their hearts would already be engaged. Why should they be punished with a lifetime of heartbreak?"

"And why should you be the martyr?" He opened one cataract-covered eye. "Do you not deserve to be happy?"

"I deserve better than a man who, though he tries to hide it, yearns for another woman, and who, because of the nature of things, is forced to remain by my side. Only I can feed his needs."

He clicked his tongue a few times. "We shall see."

She stood up, placing the knife into her large bag, and gave her blind mentor a kiss on his silver-bearded cheek. She unfolded the knitted blanket on the back of his chair and placed it over his lap. "I will visit you before I leave."

4

"And after?"

"We both know the answer. I will come if I am still able."

"And if you are not."

"If it goes as we suspect, I will not be permitted to come back through the portal. I will take the ferry to one of the family safe houses." She shuddered, but there was nothing to be done about it. She had to release her husband's bond so he could find contentment, his happiness worth any price. Some days she even believed it.

Allias humphed. "It would be a great shame to lose one of the great curse breakers."

"Perhaps this was always what the Fates had in mind."

"The Syndicate will not be happy."

"I couldn't give two fucks if they are happy or not. The Rowan's owe no allegiance to them anymore."

"Now you sound like Sarka and Rekkus rolled into one." The old man got to his feet. "Trust your heart, Janessa. Because sometimes our head get in the way."

***

"She wants to what?" Sarka screeched. "No vamp is worth the price she will pay!"

"Sarka, Janessa needs our support in this. I cannot believe she has come to this decision lightly. She loves her husband...." Cemil protested.

"Undead or not." Cyrus shrugged. He only wanted his cousin to be happy.

"How many vamps are they bringing in their

entourage?" Rekkus asked in his usual getting-down-to-business tone. Likely, he sought the answers he needed so he could get the hell out of there. Lucky bastard.

"Is that all you ask about Rekkus?" Sarka's eyebrows shot to her hairline.

"It's *all* that concerns me at the moment." Rekkus turned his attention to Sage who flipped through a book of herbs in the corner. "How many vamps?"

"Three. And two are quite old. Livia and her husband Emil can go weeks without feeding. She has assured us they will need very little while they are here."

"And Silvano?"

Cyrus clenched his mug as an awkward silence came over the room at Sarka's question. Who would finally answer it? When no one did, he mouthed the word chicken at his brother before answering. "He feeds from Janessa."

"She's his feeder? Oh, this gets better and better." Sarka threw her hands.

"She is his bonded mate. You above all others understand some exceptional witches get a great deal of power from the act." Sage never lifted her soft, calm voice to be heard. "I believe it seemed like the ideal situation. They both got what they needed."

"So, to reiterate, I don't need to worry about humans being fed on? Good. Then I don't need to sit through the rest of this." Rekkus stood, daring anyone to waylay him. No one spoke, but Cyrus knew Rekkus hadn't expected anyone to. Fatherhood had made the tiger both more and less understanding.

Cemil rubbed his head. "There is one more thing.

It is possible when she has finished her ritual she will need to leave the island via the ferry."

"She will be in no shape to go anywhere for a week or two after. I have arranged for one of the tree houses to be refitted for her needs for those two weeks." Sage looked up from her book.

Sarka stood. "I need to get some things ready for her. I'll be in my workroom. No one should disrupt me."

Cyrus shuddered. This week would be harder than he expected. Every year, the anniversary of the massacre was difficult, but, this year, they would lay the souls to rest. Grant the souls one simple request, whatever would give them the peace to pass on. He would give anything for the three sisters who left this earth before their time.

"Cyrus, are you all right?" Cemil placed a hand on his brother's shoulder.

Damn it! Could no one have a thought or feeling on this damned island without everyone knowing it first. "You already know I am not. So why bother even asking?"

"Out of respect and to give you the chance to say it's none of my damned business." Cemil remained monotone, void of the overwhelming emotions his empath sibling always experienced.

Great. He couldn't even be pissed without his brother understanding. "My pain is no more or less than anyone else in the family. Even Rekkus feels our pain with us. But this is the first time their souls will be able to tell us what they need to be at peace."

"And you worry they blame you."

"Why not? I blame me. If not for—"

"Fate." Sage flipped another page. "You cannot

be blamed for your powers. Any more than Janessa can be held to the bonds fate has handed out."

Cyrus nodded, but no one seemed to understand not only the upcoming ceremony worried him. But the dread of what his slain sisters would ask him to do. Cyrus excused himself in search of Rekkus. If anyone would shake him out of his pity party, it was him. No one knew better than he the pain of losing your family in a massacre. Rekkus had lost his entire family at the hands of his mother's cooking. With the remaining six of the original coven coming through the portal in the upcoming days, things were bound to get...emotional.

He passed Myron who kept her gaze on her cards. "Providing the cards don't change, the rooms are set. With every cabin and room on the island full, changing might not be easy to accomplish."

"Thanks, Myron."

"Cyrus?"

"Don't read me."

"Cyrus...."

"If you care at all for me, you will give me what little privacy I can find."

Myron tapped her cards in a neat pile and extended them to him. "You know I care. And I don't need cards to know you are in pain. Perhaps you could help Dana with the babies."

Cyrus closed Myron's fingers over the cards and pushed them back toward her. Her suggestion was a nice way of saying she knew he found peace in the babies' innocence and, with that peace, some sense of connection.

***

Silvano Božović stepped through the portal, cracked his neck to ease the ache, and moved forward. The first of the nightwalkers to come through, hell, the first one in line at the capital, he sniffed the air. Janessa had arrived first, he could smell her. The need to touch her grew strong. He would have to greet his parents later. They would sense his need and it would only cause more strife between them and Janessa. They already disliked Janessa and his all-consuming passion for her didn't help.

He was stronger than this unbearable bonded desire he had for her. Balling his fist, he waited for the need to pass. It wouldn't pass completely, but the roar of his blood would ease. He learned from others' mistakes. His grandfather had let his need for his bond mate dictate everything, and the hive had suffered, continued to suffer. His step-grandmother, for lack of a better word, had manipulated Valco and many family heirlooms were lost.

Imagine his surprise when he found his girlfriend's family possessed them. Worse to discover the witch in line to inherit them was also his bond mate. Nothing he could do would get them back. And the protection spell placed on the relics prevented any vampire from touching them. Thus his family could no more claim their birthright as the true rulers of their realms than they could stroll in the daylight.

In one fell swoop, he'd lost a woman he thought he might have a future with, been bonded with a woman he didn't trust, and discovered what his father feared—they couldn't prove their blood rights. If anyone questioned their ability to rule, and grumbles had been brewing for decades, they would lose everything.

"Welcome to the Wiccan Haus, Silvano." The deep purr of the black tiger prince rumbled through him.

"Rekkus." Silvano bowed. The tiger may not have claimed his birthright, but he would show him the respect due. Rising, he put out a hand. Even at his full six foot three inches, Rekkus still towered over him. "I'm thankful to see a familiar as well as friendly face."

Rekkus returned the handshake. "How long has it been?"

"Long before either of us bonded. I understand your mate has blessed you with a litter. *Gratulálok.*"

"You must come to our place and meet them all." Rekkus turned back to the portal as it groaned open again. "We have a great number of paras coming through tonight. We can catch up after dinner. You're in room nine, second floor. No need to check in. Your mate already did so."

The large man in black went back to greeting arriving guests, although with less friendliness than he had greeted Silvano. Rekkus was well-known in the para world for his surly attitude. Only a select few ever got to know the multi-layered man beneath. As for the large number of para guests, Silvano had figured it would be the case when his bond mate requested they come to the island this week. Though he saw no reason to be there for the healing aspects of the resort, Janessa did need to attend the service for their fallen coven. As he could go no more than a few waking hours without her presence, he would have to accompany her. She believed he could go a few days, and he didn't correct her belief. He wished to give her no more knowledge of the damned power she had over him.

He was pleasantly shocked when she suggested his parents come to ease some aches his father suffered. His parents had never been in her corner. In fact, they often spoke about their dislike for his witch, as if he had a choice in the matter. As fate would have it, they had spent the minimum amount of time in each other's presence. The door to his room was open. He paused outside.

"Come in, Silvano." Janessa's voice came from what sounded like the bathroom due to the echo.

The pleasant smells of fresh-cut herbs and flowers assailed his senses as he crossed the threshold into the rich, deep-burgundy room. Candle sconces on all four walls lit the space. He removed his sunglasses and relaxed. "Have you been here long, Janessa?" He came toward her and brushed his fingers against her shoulders, bared by the low neckline of her dress.

"I came through this morning. I had some things to prepare for the week." She cast up at him a sad little smile. Her dull and lifeless eyes lacked their usual brightness. He had noticed her absence of cheer as of late, but chalked it up to the coming week. But, in fact, the light had been ebbing since their last blowout fight.

"You are enchanting tonight." She showed far more skin than she usually did.

She lifted her hand to him turning it to expose the inside of her wrist, inked with the Rowan family tree tattoo. "You are hungry. I can feel your need. Eat."

God, he hated this need she alone could meet. As if it weren't bad enough he could have sex with no other than his bonded mate. Oh, he could feed off others, but it was like a man who had dined in a world class restaurant then been told he must eat from the dog bowl. Only the taste of her would do. And she offered him her wrist, not her neck or, his favorite spot to feed, her inner thigh.

"I mean no offense, my love. Dinner is served in thirty, and we are required to be there."

My love. Weeks had passed since those words had passed her lips. He hadn't realized he enjoyed them until she took them away. He couldn't blame her. "Of course. How selfish of me. This weekend, the last thing you need is intimacy with me. I am here to support you."

With those words, he bit down on her wrist. His tongue knew which vein to drink from and led his teeth to where to pierce. With a hiss, she tensed. He let the thick, red fluid enter his mouth. When she finally moaned, he swallowed and sucked, careful not to drink too much or take her too far into the sensual haze his feeding created.

Drawing only enough to appease his hunger, he licked the two holes shut and kissed her skin. "Thank you."

She shrugged, taking her hand from his and focusing on her image in the mirror to fix her makeup. "It is the least I can do for you."

And there it was. This new stance she had taken. "Are we going to go through this every sunset?"

"I don't know what you mean." She paused mid mascara swipe.

"The hell you don't. You are my bond mate, not a

servant or employee."

"I'm your bond mate not by your choice. I'm here to feed you, to take care of your 'needs.' Is that not what a servant does?"

"I do not employ you—"

"I get my payment through the surge to my powers. Call it bartering, call it payment. We are but two unlucky—" She stormed toward the door, and he could have sworn he smelled her tears, but when she turned back to him, her cheeks were dry. "Actually, if you are accommodating, sex would be a wonderful diversion while we are here."

"I am ever yours." He gave a mock bow. He hated this pain she felt, but he knew not how to fix the situation. "I understand there are some rules I am to sign."

"Yes, the list is on the desk."

He crossed the room, lifted the pages, and started to read. "In blood?"

"It's Sarka. Of course you will be signing in blood."

Sarka Rowan was well-known in the Nightwalker community. First, because of the great love affair she'd enjoyed with another vamp and now for her sudden change of heart and great hatred of their kind. He picked up the silver pen and ignored the sting running through his fingertips.

The Rules

You shall use no glamour on any human to get them to take you to the human floor.

No human who has not signed a contract may be used as a meal.

"Have you signed a contract?" He knew for a fact Sarka would love nothing more than to throw his ass through the portal at sunrise.

"We are bond mates. The rule doesn't apply to us." She laced her boot but never looked in his direction.

You will be back in your room at thirty minutes to sunrise.

No scaring the humans.

You will come to the dining room for dinner every night, no exceptions.

The rules continued for three pages and ended with, *If any of these rules are broken, your fangs will be physically removed by security and handed to you in a jar as your ass is kicked off the island.*

He pricked his finger with the end of the pen and signed his name. He turned to find Janessa staring at him in the odd manner she employed now and again lately. As if studying his every line. "Are you well?"

She blushed. "Fine. Come on, we should head downstairs."

"We still have ten minutes. But, if you wish to go, we shall."

"Thank you." The speed of her steps increased as if she had a tremendous need to get out of the privacy of their room. To his surprise, a great many people congregated at the end of the hallway for the lift to take them to the dining room.

After handing off the signed contract to Myron the Romany at the reception desk, he entered the dining room with an arm intimately wrapped around his wife's waist. He knew to stay in the darker-green area; staff left no trick unused to keep it so. The humans dined with sterling silver forks and spoons, anathema to the weres. They dipped their bread in oil laced with fresh garlic, which vamps were known to avoid, and cut their meat with iron knives to keep the fairies at bay. No superstition seemed to be left out.

"Janessa." A blond warlock with hair down to his waist came up and enveloped her in his arms. "I'm sorry I wasn't here to greet you this morning."

"Cemil." She greeted him with warmth long absent in her. "Sage met me when I arrived, and then Cyrus and I lunched together. They said you were working with someone."

"I assume this is Silvano?"

"Forgive me. Where are my manners? Silvano, this is my cousin Cemil."

Silvano gave a short bow. "A pleasure. I have heard a great many things. Your talents are legendary." He spoke the truth. One of the great empaths, Cemil would have gone far in their world had he not retreated here.

"As I have of you. Your ability to keep peace is no small feat. Welcome to our home. I hope you have a productive stay." His friendly smile faded as he faced his cousin. All too quickly, Cemil's brow marred with concern. "Janessa, we might need to have a session tonight."

She nodded, her shoulders slumping wearily.

"My sweet, we must get you some protein. I fear I feed too deeply."

She shook her head placing a hand on his chest. "No, really, you were very gentle. But I am hungry."

"Have a seat. I will have someone bring you something immediately. What would you prefer?" Cemil gestured for one of the serving staff to approach.

"Steak, rare, if you please."

"Coming right up. And for you, Silvano. Would

you like some *wine* perhaps?"

He shook his head. He had no interest in drinking the blood of a stranger, his thirst eased only by the busty redhead he led to the far table. Once she'd devoured half her steak, and not likely to pass out on him, as she had done so in the early stages of their relationship, he assessed the room. A very long time since he had been in the presence of humans, it amazed him they didn't try to cross over to the darker-green side, although they didn't understand the danger they might be in.

He waved over one of the security working the room. "Will Rekkus be coming up for dinner?"

"No, milord. He dines with Ms. Dana and the children for their evening meals," the other man, part fae by the smell of it, answered before continuing between the tables.

"I met Rekkus's mate this morning," Janessa said between bites. How he loved to watch her eat. Loved to see her color brighten and smell her blood thicken. When she next spoke, genuine joy filled every word. "The cubs might be the cutest babies I have ever seen."

Addicting. How long since she displayed anything but melancholy, he'd almost forgotten the pleasure he derived from her happiness. "Were they in human form?"

"Two were. According to Dana, the boys are very strong for their age, but the girl is still small, so she is having a harder time holding forms."

"I had wondered at the strange scent when I approached you tonight." He raised his nose as he sniffed in the intoxicating rich aroma.

She cocked her head to the side, a half-formed

smile upon her lips. "Smell?"

"Mother's milk. Your maternal instincts awoke this afternoon. The scent is quite heady. Perhaps, when we leave, we should start a conversation about getting you with child."

He had sensed her growing maternal needs over the last two years but done his best to ignore them. Still adjusting to being bonded, fatherhood had not been on his agenda. Unlike his grandfather who had a Dhampir bride to reproduce with before a bond mate appeared. He could not say what characteristics any child of theirs would have. But, so far, all offspring of vampires remained nightwalkers.

Her smile faded at his words. Not the result he had expected.

"There you are." The voice sang over him, and he searched Janessa first with surprise then confusion before switching his attention to the owner of the voice. "Silvano."

Standing, he instinctively stopped Narsaria from throwing her arms around him. It would be disrespectful for his past lover to show such familiarity in public, but his soul also fought the idea of anyone but his bond mate touching him in such a manner. "What are you doing here?"

"Janessa invited me."

"She did?" How unlike her. Janessa's irrational jealously of her sister had started many of the fights between them. His bond mate shrugged before getting up and offering air kisses to a stepsister she didn't particularly like let alone trust.

"Glad you could make it." He sensed no sarcasm in her voice, only some foreign resignation.

"I was so shocked when you invited me I almost

didn't come for fear of some sort of setup." She took a seat and ordered a salad before turning her attention to him. "But Janessa has never been the unkind type, and as I have never been invited to any of the Rowan witchy stuff, this seemed too good an opportunity to pass up."

"Narsaria, please remember there are humans present who do not know of our world."

"Oh, right," she continued, a few degrees quieter. "Forgive me. Anyway, a free trip to the Wiccan Haus, I would be a complete idiot to decline."

He could almost hear Janessa biting her tongue before he realized he had no idea what the week cost them as no bill had crossed his desk. His wife had some money of her own, not much, but enough, and rarely if ever did she spend any of his bankroll on anything except when it involved his house. "Who is paying for this, Janessa?" He kept his voice neutral.

"There is never a charge for family to come to the Wiccan Haus." She brought a glass of wine to her lips, neatly sidestepping his questions.

"Nessa," he murmured close to her ear.

"You are considered family as well."

He nearly flinched at the subtle barb. He might be considered family by her kin, but no one from his family had treated her with anything but disdain. "Yes, but my parents and your stepsister are not."

"I paid for all three trips. What does it matter?"

"Let me cover my mother and father's visit." He knew asking to cover Narsaria would only start an argument, and his mate's mental state was too frail to deal with a debate right now. He hoped being near family after the séance would help her mend. When they first met, she was a spitfire, full of light and energy. Now he didn't know if she could make it through the coming full moon.

Lifting a hand, she shook her head. "Please don't take my blessing. This is my gift to everyone. I don't want you to pay any more than I want their thanks. They don't know and it's the way I would like to keep it."

He knew for a fact a stay here very likely drained the meager funds she had available to her, but they could discuss it later. His attention moved to the hand now resting on the crook of his arm. Without thinking, he removed Narsaria's grip, placing her hand on the table in front her. Although he wanted to find out what went on in his wife's beautiful head, he couldn't turn away from Narsaria without being completely rude. Yet he hadn't remembered her chatter annoying him so much.

Torn between social etiquette bred into him through centuries, and dealing with a mate who didn't have much to say, he did the only thing he could. He grabbed his mate's hand with a squeeze before returning his attention to a conversation in which he had no interest.

Chapter Two

*S*tep one: *You must see the object of your mate's affection and your mate together, and you must be in physical contact with your mate. Say the words "I release you." These words do not need to be spoken loudly, but they must be released into the universe.*

"I release you." Janessa eyed Silvano and Narsaria together.

Except for a quick intake of breathe, Silvano seemed unaware she had initiated the breaking of their bond. But while he seemed no worse for wear, her heart squeezed in her chest. Only when she gasped did Silvano turn to her, his brow furrowed in concern.

"*Feleség,* what is it?"

She couldn't catch her breath, as if drowning on air. She shook her head, pushing the chair from the table, yet his hold on her tightened. As she blindly turned, a pair of strong arms enveloped her. Only then did he release her hand. "Breathe, little cousin. Breathe with me if you have to."

She nodded into Cyrus's protective embrace,

burying her head into his chest. Shudders racked her body as cold shards of ice shot through her veins. Pain ripped through her like a hurricane ripping apart a paper sign. She had been warned but nothing prepared her, nothing could have.

"Did you really think this was the right location to begin your quest?" Cyrus's voice held love with no admonishment. A simple question as he laid a kiss on the top of her head.

What to say? She had to start it when they were all three in the same vicinity and when her mate grabbed her, the stars had aligned. She heard the growl behind her. The predator in her mate had awakened. The hair on the back of her neck rose and her blood boiled, alerting her to his mood and needs. He had never been like this with her before. But she had never given him reason to be. Yet their connection had never been of this sort either. Tonight could simply be explained as social etiquette. One did not embrace another in public when others could see, especially one of the opposite sex.

"Down bloodsucker," Sarka's voice commanded, and she was at once ripped from the arms of one cousin into another. "Your heart is too soft, Nessa. Must I always protect you?"

Unlike Cyrus's protective, brotherly embrace, Sarka's was tight like that of a long lost friend. She wrapped her arms around her corseted cousin and squeezed. "Yes, and I will always be there to pick up your pieces when you fall apart."

"You promised to keep our secret between us," Sarka teased. She pulled back to take a good look at her. "How is it you get more beautiful? It's not fair, you know. People spend hundreds to get your kind of red from a bottle and you wake up every morning with it."

"The dark ones." Silvano's voice was low as he reached out to touch Janessa. Touching her both to reassure himself and let her know everything was all right.

"My apologies." She stepped back, not close enough to give in to her need to have his arms around her, but enough the pull between didn't seem so taut. "Silvano, my cousins Cyrus and Sarka."

"Your reputation precedes you both." He gave a low bow.

"As does yours, vampire prince," Sarka sneered.

"Vladamire sends his regards," Silvano sneered back.

Turning to Silvano, Janessa pushed against the hard wall of his chest. "No, please don't."

"Vlad can rot in eternal hell as can you, you bloodsucking fucking—"

"Enough, Sarka." Cyrus grabbed his sister around the waist, lifting her as if she weighed no more than a toddler, and removed her from the dining room. Only then did Janessa realize they had made quite the scene.

"You had to go there, didn't you? You couldn't help throwing the knowledge you are friends with her ex in her face, not even caring it would hurt someone I love."

"Yet she can insult me who you claim to love as well. You wonder why I put little stock in an emotion I have little faith in." She stepped away, trying hard to hide the hurt those words caused in her. "Nessa, I shouldn't have said that."

She waved him away "Why? You spoke truth. It's

not as if your feelings for me have ever been a secret to anyone, particularly me."

Sage entered the room and made a beeline for their table. Her aura glowed yellow, as a halo around her head, a glowing sun in the softly lit room. "Wow. I haven't seen Sarka so worked up in ages. Well done, Silvano. Don't let her treat you like a floor mat. No one wins, then."

"You must be Sage."

"Guilty as charged." The joy of life lit up the smaller woman's eyes.

"My understanding is, of all the Rowan siblings, you have never been guilty of anything but kindness to all."

"I would like to hope so, but even I have a moment of bitchiness now and again. Just as Sarka has her moments of kindness."

"A yin to your yang."

"Exactly. Would it be all right if I stole your wife for an hour or two? I sense her chakras might be misaligned from the portal. I would like to make sure you are 100 percent before the solstice."

"I would leave her in your safe hands gladly."

"Good. Besides, I do believe I saw your parents in the lobby. They are begrudgingly on their way in. I do not believe they understood how serious we are about everyone coming for dinner."

"They didn't...."

"Stop worrying, Nessa. We didn't even have to get Rekkus to go and get them from their room. Ah, here they are now."

Great, the only people she wanted to see less than Narsaria would be her in-laws who liked her less than anyone she knew. Plastering on the all-too-familiar appearance of happiness, she steeled herself for their glowers and comments about how the Fates got it all wrong.

"Be good," Salvino whispered next to her ear.

"Me?"

"Much better to be angry at me than dreading dealing with my oppressive parents. No?"

She scowled. "You have serious issues."

Every now and then this softer side would come through, giving her a glimpse of what it could be like with him. These moments both made her decision to leave him harder, yet cemented her resolve. He'd acted like this before she had come on the scene. But with the tension between her and his parents, the issues with Narsaria, and knowing his true desires, she couldn't turn a blind eye.

"Well, well what a surprise. Narsaria, I had no idea you would be here. I now have someone to keep company with while I relax this week." The nightwalker queen embraced Narsaria with loving affection. "Silvano neglected to tell me you would be here as well."

"I didn't know. I am as surprised as you." He left Janessa's side to greet his parents.

Sage wrapped an arm around her, urging her to leave the room. "Come on. You owe them no loyalty."

Surprised to hear the statement from the kindest of all the Rowans, Janessa could only gape. Sage was light, not only in complexion, but also in her ways of dealing with the world. The first of the cousins to smile again after the massacre and the first to practice her talents. For weeks after the death of the Rowan sisters, the remaining coven members had appeared to the world as broken, Cyrus the worst, and, if not for Rekkus, she honestly believed her cousin would have hurt himself or others. Yet, Rekkus, a man who had borne witness to the murder of his own family, provided stability her family needed when the ground felt like quicksand.

"They would have had you standing there like a beggar hoping for a handout. You are better. Besides, since you have made your decision, their opinion of you should no longer matter. You no longer need to spend an eternity trying to get into their good graces."

"Thank you."

"Whatever for?"

She pulled her cousin into a tight embrace. "For putting a silver lining on every gray cloud."

"It's always there, but sometimes you have to close your eyes to see it."

As they strolled a bit farther away from the Haus, the lights faded until only the stars led their way. "Where are we going?"

"I can think of no better way of realigning a chakra than playing with some babies." Her whole face lit up as they came over a hill to the inlet housing two cabins.

"Am I the excuse to see the babies this late at night?"

Dana exited her cabin and handed the blond-haired Kalina, her squirming baby girl, into Sage's arms. "She needs no excuse. Thank you for coming down."

The new mother of three took a single step inside and returned a second later with Brynn, one of the dark-haired twin boys, in her arms. Before Janessa could even stretch out her arms to offer to take the boy, he was shoved at her. His big, golden eyes stared up at Janessa before he cuddled into the nook of her neck.

Dana sighed. "I need a few minutes. Sage, would you mind?"

Sage nodded and indicated the two babies. "Where is Rhys?"

"Inside with Rekkus."

Dana's shoulders drooped, and the dark circles under her dulled brown eyes showed her lack of sleep.

Sage offered her a soft smile. "I can stay as long as you need and would be happy to come down and help tomorrow."

"You are too sweet, and, yes, that would be appreciated." Dana rubbed a hand over her face. "Right now, it's the witching hour for them. Literally." She chuckled, but Janessa could hear the fatigue in her voice.

"Go soak in the hot spring." Sage tickled the baby in her hands.

Dana passed them both a grateful smile. "It's not that I don't love them...."

"Dana, stop already. We understand. Three babies who aren't shifting from human to tiger would be a lot to handle for any mom, triplets who are and have figured out they are mobile in animal form virtually impossible."

Janessa watched Dana walk away from the house. Each step seemed to take such effort to make. "Is it safe, I mean I know the island is as safe as it can be, but should she be going off by herself? What if she falls asleep in the water? The poor mama is exhausted."

"Dana is never truly alone much like Cyrus, besides I doubt she will be alone long. We try hard to help, but we can't feed them. Only she can. To be human and have to feed three shifting babies is a huge effort. It is sometimes hard for her to get all the calories and protein she needs in a day. She has lost thirty pounds and shows no signs of stopping." Once Dana moved out of sight, Sage turned to the cabin door. "Let's see if Rekkus needs a break."

Entering the quaint living room, she found the large tiger lying in the middle of the room with all the furniture pushed back and a tiger cub pulling at his ear. Rekkus rolled the cub and shifted before his son could reach him again. Janessa turned her head, blushing as the giant man stood naked before them.

"It's safe. I'm dressed now." He pulled the cord on his sweatpants tight before bending over to pick of the cub. He made a sound deep in his throat, forcing the cub to shift. The naked curly-haired chubby baby looked at the two women then up at his dad, his lower lip wobbling before a sob left his lips. "Let me put a nappy on this one. Come on, Rhys."

"Did we interrupt?" Janessa whispered.

"He can hear you." Sage rolled her eyes and mouthed the word duh. "This is the time Rekkus uses to help them shift. He keeps hoping if he can wear them out, they can get some sleep."

"How's it working?"

"It's not." Rekkus sat back down on the floor, allowing his son to freely explore in human form. "Where did Dana head?"

"The hot spring." Sage cast him a cheeky grin.

After Rekkus growled low and so intense it hit her in the pit of her stomach, Janessa offered, "Why don't you join her?"

Rekkus's golden eyes glowed with passion. "You wouldn't mind."

"Think of it as a date night." Sage nodded toward the door. "Everyone needs a date now and again. She isn't exactly expecting you."

"But I sense she needs you." Janessa had sensed it very strongly.

The were-tiger didn't need another minute. He kissed his kids and ran out the door. She sensed more than saw his shift before he left his front porch.

"Those two had better be careful they don't create another litter tonight."

Janessa closed her eyes and reached out in the night with her powers. "They are safe, at least for the time being."

As Sage said, nothing lifted the soul more than holding an infant. And she did feel more at peace. Her heart still ached, but holding the baby girl who had now snuggled into her arms playing with her hair, a lightness came over her.

"Dana truly loves Rekkus, doesn't she?"

"She does. We watched her fight her attraction and watch with bated breath as Rekkus tried to fight fate, but, in the end, they both found they loved each other. We have all known Rekkus so long I don't think it ever occurred to any of us he wouldn't continue with his tomcat bachelor ways forever. When Dana stepped off the ferry, I never imagined she would never leave."

"What if she hadn't wanted to stay on the island?"

"You're asking would Rekkus have left with her?"

Janessa nodded.

Sage shook her head. "No. He was prepared to let her go. I'm not certain she would have stayed away longer than a week, but he made the decision not to leave Cyrus unprotected."

"And in Rekkus's world, only he can protect Cyrus." The Rekkus she had known growing up protected her cousin even before the Syndicate appointed him to do so.

Sage focused on the door with a frown. "I think in any world only he is capable of protecting my family. If not for him *that* night...."

Janessa reached out and grabbed Sage's free hand. No words were needed as they both let the grief of the loss of the three Rowan sisters wash over them. Even the boy babies calmed. But the little girl's lower lip trembled and her aura turned the lightest of blues. The room temperature dropped thirty degrees, leaving her brothers shivering in the cold.

Pressing the baby to her chest to sooth her, Janessa lightened her voice. "Sage?"

"Her powers are still forming, but we think she is a partial empath and, like her aunt before her, will be a weather alterer. So far, it is affected by her moods, but when Dana was pregnant, the weather would change with hers."

A knock at the door broke the tension. Sage got up to open it and threw it wide open before saying anything, Janessa didn't have to turn to know who stood at the threshold. The draw to invite him in was no less strong although more painful than usual. Sage, sensing something, turned and whispered, "Be strong. The pain is there to make you not want to break the link."

She nodded, trying to catch her breath. As if

trying to help, the little girl in her arms snuggled closer and cooed.

"I can't let you in. I hope you understand."

"I do. Rekkus's mate is human. I can imagine her ideas of nightwalkers run toward what the movies have told her."

"Those and Sarka."

"Ouch." He glanced over Sage's blonde head to Janessa. Although she focused on the downy head of the baby in her arms, she could feel his hunger as his gaze washed over her. "I was worried about my mate. Her sadness crashed through me like a tsunami a few minutes ago."

"As you can imagine, the upcoming days are a mix of sadness, survivor's guilt, and, ironically, joy."

"*Priyatel*?"

"I'm fine," she mumbled into the soft curls, breathing in the fresh scent of baby shampoo.

"She's fine," Sage echoed.

"I heard her." His voice held frustration, the desire to touch her, to be closer. The invisible barrier protecting the house from him and his kind impeded his need. "Can you not face me?"

She did and she knew he saw a sadness she couldn't hide, only thankful he didn't know the depths of her despair, or the reason. As they had never done the full blood exchange, he couldn't read her mind. And although she had always hoped one day he would ask her to complete the final portion of their bond, current circumstances made her thankful he hadn't. Had he asked her for her heart's desire, she would have agreed, even knowing deep inside he wished he was with another. Leaving him would have been virtually impossible.

Her pain already unbearable, she couldn't imagine what she would have felt after the blood bond.

"Janessa." His rich, sexy voice caressed her like silk, pulling her to him. On feet not working on their own volition, she closed the distance between them, his call hard to fight.

Sage stepped into her path. "No."

"It's okay. He is still my mate. He cannot hurt me."

"My *mate* is right, and you know it." Barely contained hostility laced his voice. He would not believe anyone dared to come between him and his mate. The tie between them snarled them mind and body if not yet soul.

Sage didn't budge but raised her voice. "You do not mean to, but you do without knowing it."

"Sage, stop, please. I know you love me."

Sage bowed her head but not in time to hide the tears in her eyes.

"Will they mind if I take the baby outside?"

Sage shook her head. "The babies are in no danger."

Janessa took a stabilizing breath before crossing the threshold. She held the baby close with one hand and brushed her lover's cheek, giving him, no, each of them, the connection they craved. "Better?"

"Hardly enough." He glanced at Sage who moved deep into the room to offer them a degree of privacy. "Why do I feel there is a deep undercurrent on the island that I have a great deal to do with but know nothing about."

Shrugging, she eased into one of the Adirondack chairs as the baby giggled, grabbing a handful of hair.

"We are bonded and I am family, making you part of the circle here. You having never been around my more caring side of the family, have never witnessed anyone worry about me. These are my family, my coven."

"I am your family."

"Fate decreed it, not choice. Even if I weren't born to the Rowans, they would choose me. Myron and Rekkus have chosen me. They all protect me, and they feel my pain as if it is their own."

"And what pain do they feel, *zvyozdochka*?"

His Star. She almost told him—a hairsbreadth from yelling at him—her pain resulted from having the bad luck to be bonded to a man who tolerated her while cursed with an attraction bordering on addiction. "My pain is knowing I will speak to three family members for the last time. It, in part, will be my actions allowing them peace to move on."

"Like Rekkus's sister did in choosing to return in the form of the child in your arms?"

He so rarely used his gift in her presence, she almost forgot his depth at knowing souls. Not a soul path who read a soul's feeling or purpose, but he knew their pasts. In part because his people were considered soulless, they seemed more in tune with what they lacked. "Yes, like Eiriana."

The baby reached up and placed an openmouthed kiss on her chin.

"Oh, I love the sugar." She giggled, allowing herself to feel the joy of the soft innocent embrace.

"You appear almost happy. I cannot remember the last time I sensed your joy."

"It is easy to enjoy such innocence." She met his eyes over the head of the baby. A few minutes of happiness wouldn't change her course of action but perhaps made it more bearable.

"I see you have met my pride and joy," Rekkus purred from the darkness. The baby immediately turned and squealed in the direction of her daddy. Rekkus swooped the child up in his arms to be rewarded with a fit of giggles. "Are you loving Auntie Janessa?"

Janessa could barely believe she faced the same tiger she had known all her life. Then she saw Dana standing behind her mate, so much calmer than a half an hour before. She brushed her lips against Rekkus's bare shoulder, a simple gesture which spoke of their connection and passion.

"Better?" Janessa could read the other woman's aura which glowed significantly brighter than it had when she left, but she needed to say something to fill the silence.

Even in the darkness, a slight hint of a blush could be seen warming Dana's cheeks. "Much."

"She missed her babies so we had to come back." He cast a long suffering glance at the mother in question. "Silvano, I don't believe you have met my wife."

Silvano marveled at the tiger shifter cuddling his infant daughter against his chest. "I have not had the pleasure."

"I'm glad to meet you, Silvano. Rekkus has spoken much about you. Please excuse me, but I need to feed my babies." She rubbed the curly head of the baby in her mate's arms as a cry rent the night. "I think I'll start with the boys."

Janessa shivered, and Rekkus nodded to the

warmth of the living room. "Come on in. It's warmer inside."

Janessa moved ahead into the cottage, but Silvano paused outside the door. "Are you sure you want to invite me in, Rekkus? Your human bride...."

"Dana?" Rekkus threw the question over his shoulder.

From an unseen corner of the house, Dana answered, "Please. If the most protective tiger in the world is letting you into this house with his babies, I have nothing to fear from you."

"Very open-minded." Silvano passed over the threshold into the friendliness of the bright room. The cottage, though small and certainly not what one would expect the Tiger Prime would inhabit, exuded love and security. Compared to the stuffy and proper atmosphere of his chateau, he could understand why Janessa might be drawn to this place.

The room was in disarray, toys scattered around. To cross the room he would have to cross the minefield of wooden blocks, stacking toys, and stuffed animals. With the exception of a wicker basket with *Cyrus Only* written on a slate tag attached to its side, nothing in the immediate vicinity appeared to be in its place.

Dana must have followed his gaze. "Please excuse the mess. With three to keep up with, feed, change, and keep occupied, housework falls by the wayside."

"It's not as if she doesn't have a team of cleaning crew members simply begging to help," Sage mumbled from her seat on the floor.

"Sage," Rekkus admonished before pushing the table back into place, lining the legs up to the indentations in the carpet.

Janessa whispered into his ear, "Apparently, she wants to do as much as possible on her own."

"I see." His gaze met Rekkus's. The tiger shrugged before lifting a fussy baby into his arms. "I should remind you, as you appear to have forgotten, Rekkus has hearing to rival any superhero."

Janessa's mouth formed an O before a blush covered her cheeks. Unsure who chuckled first, Rekkus or him, a yawn from Dana gave him the opportunity to make their excuses. "We should leave."

"I concur." They exchanged good-byes, his bride making sure to say she would come back when the sun rose to help as needed. She needed so little rest, usually she would fall asleep a couple of hours before the sun rose and, according to their human servants, she was out and about by nine every morning. Some of his kind could stay awake after the sun rose, as long as they remained out of the sun's path, but not him. His father had managed to alter his rhythms and could stay up for as long as two hours past sunrise, depending on the season.

"I cannot imagine how they handle three babies at once."

"Well, you are lucky my kind never have more than one. Multiples are the curse of the shifters."

"I do not believe Rekkus and Dana even at their lowest moments would think those three babies are a curse."

Blighting himself, he felt her pull away, again. An unfamiliar feeling of loss had clung to him since dinner. Something had happened. He was certain. But he couldn't figure out what. The siblings knew it, too, since they had come in force to his Janessa's side. "What is going on with us?"

"What do you mean?" Though she looked him straight in the eyes, her body tensed.

"You are distant."

"I have a lot on my mind."

"With the gravity of this week, I would have thought you would be leaning on me. Allowing me to take some of the burden."

"We do not have that kind of relationship."

"If we do not try for that kind of relationship, we will never have it." He had never wanted *that* kind of relationship with her. Until a few days ago, he had been content with what they had, or so he thought. Now, he wasn't so sure.

Confusion played over her face as she locked her jaw and furrowed her brows. "What has gotten into you?"

"I do not know. But I know I am no longer content with the relationship we have. We could have more, and I see it."

"You cannot force emotions you don't feel. We have found an amicable companionship, I agree, but where we go from there...." She shrugged, turning from him. "I want to be happy, and I am no longer certain we can make each other happy."

"You make it sound like you are no longer willing to try." This explained the change he had noticed. This lack of interest in their relationship. Granted, he had not tried time and again, but, recently, he felt a tug of something he couldn't put his finger on. And he had very much noticed she hadn't expressed her feeling to him in weeks. "Is this not a place of healing? Perhaps we can work on healing our relationship. After all, this is a situation we are in together for many years to come."

"So make the best of it because there is no other choice."

"If you will."

She rubbed her temples. "I am tired and have had a full day and the next proves to be worse. If it's all the same to you, perhaps we could return to our room."

"You wish to turn in for the night?" Janessa never wished to turn in early. She loved the moon. She had told him she believed the Fates had chosen him for her because of her connection to the night. Her spells and strengths seemed intrinsically tied to the moon, like him.

"You are welcome to find your family and Narsaria. I'm certain they would welcome your company."

"I would prefer you would accompany me." He knew she would balk, but he had to say it.

"This week is hard enough without the feeling of inadequacy your family heaps on my head and the outrageous and rude flirting my stepsister does in your presence. Forgive me, but I have more than enough to deal with over the next few days."

"Why invite them? We could have easily come without any of them. Hell, not one of them needed to even know our plans. Yet, you not only invited them but paid their way. What I cannot for all the stars in the sky figure out is why you did it. Why invite people you despise to join us here in a place you hold so dear to your heart?"

"I don't hate any of them. I thought it would make you happy." Something unsaid passed over her eyes, some secret agenda. At first, he'd thought she hoped to bring the family together on this little trip. His parents expressed surprise to find she had paid for their vacation out of her private account. The one she kept her witchy earnings in. She didn't make much, but she liked having her own money to buy things so she didn't have to justify them to the accountant. Narsaria had shrugged it off with a snarky comment about how Janessa had stolen her man so a holiday was the least she could offer.

But Janessa hadn't stolen anything as much as the Fates had predetermined their mating, leaving her no more to blame for their situation than the sugar farmer is for a man getting diabetes. His bride seemed to be heaped with sins not of her making. And he'd struggled to contain his anger about the forced mating. He'd thought he had years to sow his oats. He had pined for a relationship lost that would have ended quickly enough. Only when Janessa took a step back did he see things clearly for perhaps the first time.

"A kind gesture on your part. And perhaps my parents will begin to thaw."

"There can be no thaw for any descendant of LeeAnne Rowan. What she did to your family is unforgivable and the reason I bear your parent's disdain."

"It is not your sin. You didn't curse the knife of Moshchnost. But perhaps the Fates choose you for me to help break the curse."

Her head shot up. "What do you mean?"

"Perhaps our children, with your blood running through them, will be able to wield the knife." The only thing he could think of. None of his blood could handle the knife. The very symbol of their rightful place as ruler of their people. But no one had been seen holding it in centuries, and now the whispers had started. If one of theirs didn't wield it soon, a rebellion loomed. He could sense it.

"Perhaps, but I doubt it will be in time."

She appeared so lost and guilt ridden, he did the only thing natural to them. He wrapped an arm around her, forcing her full, soft figure into tight contact with his body. His blood surged, and his carnal needs came forward. He took her lips with his, forcing her head back and her submission. She moaned, and the little sound had the alpha in him taking full charge. No way he could get them back to their room and he had no interest in trying.

He sensed no one on the path with them, but, with so many guests on the island, someone would come their way at any time. Lifting her into his arms, he walked them the five minutes to the apple orchard. The sweet blossoms' scent made his mouth water to taste his sweet bride. He laid her in a grassy area where the trees opened up enough for her to see her beloved moon. The one strength in their relationship was hot, electric sex.

He worked her neck, licking, sucking, and even scraping with his fangs but never once breaking the sensitive skin. He would feed on her, but not now. He would feed from her as she orgasmed, when her blood thickened and pumped hard.

"I hate these damned corsets." He growled against her cleavage, unable to suckle her the way he loved. But he had no patience to remove the blasted thing and even less desire to delay his journey.

Her knees fell open, accommodating his body.

39

Grabbing the hem of her skirt, he eased it up, delighting in the small goose pimples covering her soft skin. Her breath hitched as his fingers reached the band of her thong. He kneeled at her feet, pulling it off over the heeled witchy boots she wore. An image of her in nothing but these boots and her damned corset assailed him, and his hunger rose.

"What if someone comes by?"

He flashed her his best cheeky grin, the one she once admitted made her heart leap. "What if they do?"

"Silvano. I am serious. What if your parents—"

"My parents are well aware we have sex and often." He couldn't help but grin. Married for three years, she still worried. "And if someone else comes by, they will most likely not see us, or run the other direction. Now, lie back and keep your eyes on Luna above."

Warm skin against his lips fueled his need. He left a trail of tiny kisses up her thighs until he came to the apex of her legs. He breathed her scent, pausing only to adjust his hardening cock before licking her intimately until his tongue came in contact with her clit. She moaned as he circled the nub. He teased her as she laced her fingers into his hair, urging him to bring her more. He put his tongue into her and grabbed her hips to keep her in place as she arched her hips up wanting him deeper. Every time she came to the edge, he would pull her back. Delaying her satisfaction was killing him, but, for her, it would make for a more powerful orgasm.

Pants came fast, accompanied by the pleas to help her find her climax. How he longed to drag out her torture until morning, but neither of them were in the state of mind. Pausing, he stared up at her until she shifted focus from the skies above to him.

"What?" she managed.

"You are beautiful." He had told her before but never knew what beautiful was until this second. Her perfection scared the hell out of him. Crawling up her body, he released his cock and plunged it into her at the same moment he found the pulsing vein on her neck. As his teeth pierced her skin, she wrapped her legs around him and screamed out his name as she came hard. Never demure or graceful, she personified raw passion the way he wanted her. The wind around them picked up as he drew nearer to his release, and only when she went over the edge a second time did he allow himself to take his pleasure, too.

Lapping up the last of the blood drops from the pale skin, he closed the puncture wounds but did nothing to hide the bruise his aggressive feeding left. He wanted her marked by him. He wanted all who saw her to know she was his.

Chapter Three

Janessa awoke feeling sore in places not supposed to hurt. He'd ridden her harder last night than he ever had, a desperateness on both their parts. She suspected it had to do with her starting the breaking bond. Sage warned the desire to stay together would become stronger. The Fates' way of making you forget you defied them. And last night certainly had her second-guessing herself again. The power of the orgasm had made everything before it seem like nothing at all. And, for a second, they had a connection, and she had thought he would finish their mating ritual.

Relief washed over her. Although she loved him, she had to remember he did not love her and never would. He loved another. Her cousin. She made sacrifices to release them both from an eternity of loneliness. She grabbed the box in the bottom of her closet, the one holding the thing his family most prized—the Knife of Moshchnost. She next would remove the curse her ancestor has placed on the item all those years ago. She would leave her mate free to not only be with whom he chose by free will, but would, if at all possible, give him back what his family rightfully deserved—the power to rule.

Although she didn't like the treatment she received at the hands of her in-laws, they were fair and true to their people, good rulers. And no one would win if war broke out. She lingered in the room, knowing her father-in-law could remain up for up to two hours after the sun rose. Once convinced he would be asleep, she took the elevator to the first floor, waved to Myron at the front desk, and headed to the first elevator.

"Sarka is below. She has your breakfast." Myron focusing back on her cards.

Janessa chanted quietly so no one except perhaps Rekkus could have heard her. At the chime of the bell, she stepped into the rich, red velvet-walled lift. The doors closed, and it started its descent. With no buttons or call bells, only Rowan women could operate this lift. Once in use at the Rowan estate before the massacre, the siblings brought it to the island without the Syndicate's knowledge—a final safeguard to protect the witches and take them to a location where Sarka could avoid interruption.

The door opened to the cellar room. Lit by candlelight the dark room screamed Sarka and her personality. From the deep reds to the dark-gray walls, and the sign reading, *If I click my heels three times, will you disappear*? The dungeon presented exactly what everyone would believe a witch's lair to be.

"Sage has never set foot in this room."

Sarka laughed but did not stop placing gems into a necklace before her. "What gave it away?"

"Oh, just the little things like there being nothing 'light' in the room." And nothing natural, no homespun fabrics, no herbs, and certainly no sunlight. "I thought this was supposed to be both your rooms?"

"Sage is happier above the ground in her herb shack. She came down once, let the elevator doors open, beheld the room, and went right back up. She has never mentioned sharing the space again."

"What about when you have to work together?" She placed her bag on the only table cleared of all items. It didn't take a rocket scientist to tell her at which table to use.

"I go to her domain. She is far more...flexible than I am anyway."

"Say it ain't so." Janessa would bet her last penny no one would argue with the statement. "You sure you don't mind me invading your space?"

"Not at all. It will be nice to have someone I can talk with while I create." Sarka brought a Moroccan oil lantern over to Janessa's table, allowing for more light. "There are times on this blasted island I feel misunderstood."

Janessa understood oh too well. "Like, no matter what you say or do, there is always someone teaming up with someone else making you the odd woman out?"

"Exactly. The staff laugh and claim I am one of the dark ones. But, unlike the light ones, I don't have a counterpart. Sage has Cemil—they are two peas in one of her herby pods. Cyrus has Rekkus. Those two have always been Tweedle Dee and Dum."

"Rekkus has always been Cyrus's protector."

"And Cyrus makes Rekkus stop and enjoy life

sometimes. Not sure how Dana deals with not one of them but two."

"But you lost your other half that night." She didn't need to say what other night. They always referred to the night of the murder as *that night*.

Sarka paused. "As did you."

"As did I," she agreed. "But there is also Romla. She lost her second, too, poor Saffy. Speaking of which, will she be here?"

"Romla plans to arrive in the morning but will head to the conservatory until the coven meets. She doesn't want to be around anyone yet. Orion and Willow are on an assignment and will get here when they can."

"I saw Maya briefly." They had met in the library when she arrived. Maya, the true healer of the group, was neck-deep in books, determined to make Janessa's transition as easy as possible. She didn't wish to dim the baby Rowan's positivity with the knowledge nothing she did would help. "And Raine?"

"She is staying with Myron at her Caravan. She said her cards are burning, and she needed to get away from the energy in the Haus."

No one could argue there was a great deal of energy and most of it sad at the moment. Through the lump forming in her throat, she managed, "We haven't all been together since the funeral. There isn't a day that doesn't go by that I don't think I need to tell Cel something."

When Celeste died, a part of her soul died with her. She'd bet Sarka felt the same way about her sister Sandrine, the two inseparable from when Sarka was seven and Sandy five. When the murders happened, all the siblings sensed something wrong.

But Rekkus child-locked the four Rowans into the bulletproof SUV that any world leader's security team would love to get their hands on. Sage admitted the danger of the situation only sank in when Rekkus, running full speed toward their front door, stripped naked and shifted for all the world to see. And he didn't care.

No one but Rekkus knew what truly happened in the house that night. Rekkus never said and the siblings never asked. The Syndicate police arrived, followed by Special Elite Para Forces to find the three Rowans long deceased and the five assassins torn to pieces. Instead of Cyrus and his siblings, they were greeted by the seven-hundred-pound tiger.

"So tell me what you are working on." Sarka leaned over Janessa's shoulder. So deep in thought, Janessa hadn't even realized her cousin had moved from her table.

"My ancestor cursed this knife, and I would like to remove the curse."

"Is this what I think it is?" she asked in awe. There were only a handful of pieces throughout the world that had as much prestige and history behind them as the sword she held in her hand.

"Yes, and please don't start."

"Oh, I am going to start! You are about to risk losing your powers for a man you love so much you are willing to set him free. His family, who treats you like the dirt beneath their royal feet, is facing a rebellion, and you are giving them the one thing they need to hold onto their fucking kingdom."

"I am doing what is right. And if you would try to see past your bitterness, you would understand. Vlad was an ass for not standing by you when you needed him the most, but, damn it, Sarka, it was six years ago. He didn't know how to handle your depression and loss. Why does that make him any different than anyone else?"

"Because of what he did to Sage."

"Excuse me? What did he do to Sage?" Her blood ran cold.

"Fuck— Forget it."

"What am I to forget?"

Sarka leaned over the table, laying her forehead on the rough wood. "I went to his place, to ask him for help. We hadn't seen Sage in a few days and she was so depressed. You remember."

Janessa nodded and swallowed the lump in her throat. "As if the light had gone out in our world."

"Exactly. I approached Vlad's hive headquarters. I'd been there a hundred times, so I didn't think anything of walking right into his office. I caught him feeding on Sage. And not just him. She lay there glamoured while three fucking vamps fed off her pale and unresponsive body. They were drunk off her powers."

"What did you do?"

"Pulled them off her and called Rekkus. I couldn't think of anything else to do."

"But I don't understand. How could he feed off Sage? I thought you and Vlad were bond mates?"

"He had me and the whole world fooled. I thought he only fed from me. It would have been easier if he had banged someone else, but to feed off of my sister, and while she was glamoured...." Sarka wiped an angry tear away with the back of her hand. "Rekkus dealt with the hive before carrying Sage out. We took her to his place. I didn't want the others to know, to worry any more than necessary. So we nursed her back to health, and, when she woke, she had no idea what had happened to her. So I told her she was recovering from pneumonia."

"Did they...?" She let her sentence drag, unable to get the words past the bile clogging her throat.

"Feed during the blood thickening?" Sarka knew nothing made the taste sweeter for a vamp than feeding during the height of passion when the blood was the thickest and most potent. "No. I think that is the only reason Rekkus left any of them standing. With Sage in such bad shape, had he sensed they had taken advantage of her sexually, he would have killed them where they stood."

"Oh, fear not. I'll kill him the next time I see him. Or, better yet, I'll have Silvano tear Vlad limb from limb."

"In five days, Silvano will no longer be in your life."

She weaved as the blood rushed from her head. How could she have forgotten? "You're right, so it is unlikely I will see Vlad either."

"Sit. Down. Now." Sarka eased her into a chair before placing a mug of hot tea in her hands. "There is too much going on right now. Perhaps you should come back another week to complete your mating bond break."

"I cannot. I have begun the spell. I have to complete it now."

"Then forget this asinine idea of returning their butter knife."

The knife she held could cut bone. "Three. I must complete three trials this week."

"You and your affinity for numbers."

"Oh, and you haven't one? Let me count your numbered sets."

Sarka waved her off, going back to her jewelry. "We weren't talking about me. We are dealing with your issues."

"Thank the goddess. There isn't enough time in the year to deal with yours."

A spark crossed over her icy-blue eyes before Sarka broke into laughter. "I have missed you, cousin. You need to visit more."

"I might have to be here for an extended stay. Perhaps you can talk to management and get me a job."

"I might have an inside track for you." Sarka kept her eyes on her work but paused. "You are welcome here as long as you need to stay."

What she had hoped. She knew her healing would take time. Learning to adjust to the possibility of no longer having magical powers would take time, but how long did it take to mend a heart and soul ripped apart. Those questions nudged at her, but she had no answers. Only time would tell.

Chapter Four

Long before the sunset, he could wake from his slumbers to hear the sounds around him. An early warning system most of his kind possessed. They may be amazing hunters and be some of the most feared in the para world, but their strength came with great weakness while they slumbered.

These sounds were not the usual ones of his bride preparing for him to wake. She had always tried to be available to him when he first woke. Something he hadn't realized he craved until she hadn't been there to greet him as he came through the portal. She mumbled, sounds of wood moving filling the room. Had she hushed the wood? He woke with a grin. Opening his eyes, he rolled to the side to see what Janessa had gotten into.

Facing away from him, she pushed a long wooden beam into the wall only to have two more pop out in its place. The earthy scent of cedar filled the room. She placed hands on hips, staring down the wall. "Why won't you cooperate?" she demanded in a hushed voice.

"It is cooperating." He took mercy on her.

She jumped at the sound of his voice and blushed, making him hungry for her in more ways than one. "It is not. I thought maybe this wall held a secret compartment or something because of all the funky beams and things. Sarka laughed when I asked and said, 'Or something.' Blast her."

Getting to his feet, he didn't bother grabbing the clothes he had laid out the night before. "This is a feeding wall."

"Excuse me?" She jumped back, placing Silvano between her and the wall as if it would bite her. Charming she chose to hide behind the one thing in the room guaranteed to bite her. "Why would they have such a thing in here?"

"For some nightwalkers and feeders, these are part of a fetish." He moved his hand in an arc. Instantly, a half dozen boards eased out of the wall, including two at the top with leather straps attached. "You see, this is BDSM for nightwalkers and their partners."

"You can't be serious. Why would— I mean, have you— Is this something you would want to do...that we would want to do?"

"I have never thought about it, but, suddenly, I very much want to try."

"Now?" she squeaked.

"Definitely now." His cock shot to full attention.

"What do I do?" She cocked her head at the wall like it was a complicated jigsaw puzzle. He could imagine the cogwheels turning.

"First, I would recommend getting naked."

Heat entered the green pools as her pupils widened. The scent of her desire spurred on his to heights he didn't know existed. Her shaking fingers pulled at the front lacings of her corset. Unable to wait, he kneeled before her, yanking the skirt down until it puddled at the floor, followed quickly behind by her silk undies. "If you don't get your corset off you now, I will rip it from your body."

She paused, her mouth forming an O. He had never been out of control before. He'd viewed their coming together as a mutual necessity to give them both pleasure. He would feed, and she would get her power surge. This time, rather than hungry for a meal, he was sexually starved. The corset fell, leaving her clad in only a thin chemise, her nipples at full attention. Rising on his knees, he took one nipple into his mouth, sucking it through the soft fabric until she held onto him for support.

Rising to his feet, he lifted her, urging her legs around his hips, bringing him into intimate contact with the heat at the apex of her thighs. He hissed as if burned, so ready to take her like this. As he approached the wall, he pictured in his mind how he wanted her arranged, and the wall complied, beams moved and adjusted. "Put your wrists through the straps."

She reached, wrapped the soft strap around her wrist then repeated the action over her other shoulder. Gripping the straps, she took a deep breath, filling her lungs and pushing her breasts toward him.

"Now, place your foot on the board near the floor."

As he released her weight to allow her to step on the board, others moved securing her leg into place. She hesitated, and he kissed her, trying nonverbally to ease her nerves. He didn't think he could speak.

Gripping the underside of her knee, he raised the other leg, resting it on a long board. Stepping back, Janessa resembled a lowercase h, completely open to him. "Arch her back."

Immediately, he heard the boards inch out behind her, pushing her breasts out and up. "Does it hurt? Are you uncomfortable?"

Shaking her head, she blushed. "I feel laid bare. Defenseless. Nervous."

"Let me tell you what I see, Janessa. I see beauty, grace, and sensuality. You are so perfectly positioned for me right now. Every inch of you the exact match for me. Should your leg get tired, imagine the position you would prefer and the wall will assist you."

The pale skin against the dark wood highlighted every inch of her. He scored his nails over her thighs before approaching her lips, claiming her in a scorching kiss. His tongue forced hers to waltz with his. But the kiss was short lasting, as the growing desire for her would not allow him to take his time. Maybe later, maybe another night, but not tonight. He gripped her hip with one hand while running the other up her arm and interlocking their fingers.

He broke the kiss and moved to the underbust, the soft, delicate skin. "Mine," he hissed before finding the vein and latching on. She screamed out in pleasure as she fought to wrap around him to touch him more. He knew her thoughts as he fed, knew her needs and her wants and could see things in her mind much clearer than he ever had. Closing the bite marks, he moved his hips between hers. Removing one hand from the leather strap, he brought it down to his mouth, bit into her wrist, and entered her.

Silvano picked a rhythm, pounding into her with both force and care, until they both climaxed.

He supported her in his arms, careful not to step back until the boards in the walls began to move. She fell into his protective embrace. He remained inside her, unwilling to break the connection. "Are you all right?"

"Um, wow."

He chuckled. "Perhaps we can have one of these installed in our bedchamber."

She tensed her whole body, which had seconds before been limp in his arms, to strain to hear her. He thought he heard, too softly spoken to be sure, "I release you."

"What did you say?" Before he could demand to know what she meant and why her words sent ice through his veins, a loud and hard knock on the door sounded.

"Oh crap, dinner." Janessa jumped from his arms and frantically gathered her clothes strewn across the room. "Coming."

Silvano opened the door to one of the security guards sniffing the air. The distinctive scent of a were-panther met his own nostrils. "We will be down in a minute."

"My message for you is Rekkus doesn't give a damn if you have discovered the delights of the feeding wall. If you are not down in the next five minutes, he will come up and personally escort you both to the dining hall no matter what state of dress"—the large man raised an eyebrow—"or undress you might be in."

The guard turned on his heel and headed three doors down to bang on that one as well.

"I do believe our presence is required at dinner." He stopped his bride from entering the bathroom. "Don't shower. I want to smell myself on your skin tonight." He didn't say it aloud, but he wanted everyone to smell his scent on her. He wanted them to know she belonged to him.

"Are you all right?" she asked hesitantly.

"Yes. Get dressed. We don't need Rekkus coming up here."

"Worse, Sarka."

He nodded, heading to the chair with his clothes. Right now, Sarka presented the least of his worries. This growing desire to claim his mate, something he promised his parents he would never do, worried him greatly. How could he bind his life-force with the woman whose family might be the ultimate ruin of his? Loyalty and desire warred within him.

***

Step 2: You must be in intimate contact with your mate. Again, the words do not need to be spoken loud but they do need to be released into the world.

It hadn't hurt as badly the second time. The three words which had ripped her soul apart the first time merely caused a momentary heartache the second. But perhaps it offered a reprieve for the last time she muttered the words that would destroy her. This would rival any pain she could endure in life. But she no longer wished to be second best, and, although Silvano had showered her with attention here, she didn't fool herself. Once they returned to his family estate, the negative pressure from his parents would affect them again.

Yet, for a moment, she thought—no, *felt* a sizzle, a nudge to finish bonding. And she could have sworn he experienced it, too. She held her breath and prayed he would make the move. When he didn't, she knew he never would, and she knew she had to make the second proclamation.

"You are very quiet." Silvano touched her cheek, returning her attention to the table and those around them.

"I'm sure she has a great deal on her mind with tomorrow." Silvano's mother spoke with kindness she had never directed at Janessa before. "I had a long talk with Cemil this morning before we took our rest. He explained how hard the upcoming ceremony and anniversary was on all the Rowans."

Hard didn't begin to explain the depth of the strain she and the others would withstand the evening of the bonfire. But Janessa would have to cross an even greater barrier this week as well. She pushed a radish around her plate, finding it easier to focus on it than the people at her table. "One day hence, on Beltane, the veil will be the thinnest and there will be a super moon. Our powers will be at their height from 2:00 a.m. to 3:00 a.m."

"Especially for my little moon witch here." Silvano puffed out his chest in pride.

She paused shocked out of thought by the comment. "Yes, my powers are at their height tomorrow night. But it's the time for us to commune with our sisters who died and know have been unable to pass over. We will attempt to help them move on as they will do the same for us in turn. But this is a time for truths, and they will need to tell us what we do not want to acknowledge. It might be their anger, or our guilt, but we must deal in the truths tomorrow whatever they may be."

"The Rowans have invited us to observe," Silvano said.

"They did? I was unaware." Livia cast her cool dark-eyed gaze on her daughter-in-law. "But if you do not wish us there, we will respect your need. This is your ritual."

"Of course you are welcome. I'm surprised you want to be there."

"Narsaria explained to us what an honor it is to be invited and told us watching the Rowan coven in action is quite beautiful."

"I see." Not sure how to take this change of attitude toward her, Janessa took a sip of wine. As wine rarely appeared on the menu, Myron must have told someone she would need it.

"Nessa has never even let me observe before. I was shocked when she invited me! I always hoped I would get a chance to watch." She sounded like a teenager about to see her favorite rock band. "Aren't the other Rowan cousins coming? It's been years since I have seen them."

"They will be arriving at sundown tomorrow."

"Oh," Silvano's father said. "I assumed we could only travel to and from the island on Saturday."

"They are making an exception." Very few knew the portals still took paras from the Haus to the capital as needed throughout the week. Janessa didn't believe her in-laws fit in that need-to-know group.

"So why didn't you come through tomorrow, too?"

Fair question. "I have a great deal to prepare for tomorrow." More than any of them could know. Tomorrow, everything would change for all of them. She would help the dead move on, she would release her husband, and she would return the knife. So close to removing the curse, she was certain the last of the evil magic would be gone before the bonfire the next night. As the full moon rose, she would restore the knife to the family.

"Where will it be taking place?" Silvano pushed his plate toward her. "Try this. I'm quite sure it's delicious."

She didn't fight him. Her own meal held too little food to satisfy her after their lovemaking earlier. "The veil will be thinnest where the land meets the sea. But we have to stay well away from any humans who might be wandering the island at night. So they have designated the cove between Rekkus and Serena's cabins as the spot."

"I can see why." He encouraged her to eat another bite from his plate.

"I won't be available until after the ceremony as I will be fasting from sunup."

"Will that be safe?"

"It is a must."

Silvano cleared his throat. "I asked if it was safe. You need your energy tomorrow night. How will you have it if you have not eaten?"

"I'll be fine." What got into him? Not only his unusual concern, but to vocalize any care about her around his parents didn't happen. She felt like she had awoken to a new dimension.

"Nessa, where were you today? I tried finding you to take a class or two with, but the receptionist told me you were busy and no one would tell me where." Narsaria bit her lip.

Wondering if she was trying to stir the pot or simply curious, Janessa shrugged. "I spent most of the day with Sarka in her workroom."

"I'm glad I didn't find you, then. I have never met anyone as scary as her. And I have met some seedy people in my time." Her stepsister shivered dramatically.

"Sarka is simply bitter she and Vladimir didn't last." Silvano tapped the table. He disliked gossip. "He's moved on and she never has."

It took everything in her not to say something. She gripped her fork so hard the metal bent with the force. Only when Silvano eased it from her grasp did she relax. He leaned in whispering in her ear, "What is wrong?"

So many things, but in the end she chose to go with a concern outside themselves. "I found out something unsettling today."

"Share your burden with me."

"Perhaps later. This is not the time or place for it." She hoped he would listen and let it go. She didn't want to talk about it on the island or anywhere, but she didn't want Vlad getting away with what he had done. No real punishment could be assigned, not really, but Silvano and his family would stop support of his family, and, for now, she could believe it would be enough. "I need to walk the area for tomorrow's ritual. Would you like to come with me?"

He gaped. They didn't do things like this together. This time of the evening, he and his father reviewed the events happening with their people. "I would be happy to accompany you."

Happiness filled her until another voice interrupted it. "May I come along?"

Janessa couldn't help but feel the tug of resentment. Her stepsister was deliberate in all things, most especially her attention to Silvano. Janessa's husband never nay said his former lover's requests. About to say perhaps going alone would be best, she found Silvano shaking his head.

"Nessa needs quiet and peace. I am going to ensure she has both." Silvano's voice brooked no argument.

Why couldn't he do these things at home? She needed his support. Doubt filled her. Maybe he didn't still love Narsaria. Maybe they had a chance. She hadn't cast her last spell, and if she never chanted it, who knew what could happen?

Neither spoke as they strolled out of the Haus into the chilled April night air. A human couple greeted them as they passed. "Gorgeous night, isn't it?"

"It is," Silvano offered.

"I can't believe it's an early spring evening and I'm not in a coat." The woman laughed, clearly loving the island and its unusual weather. Maine evenings in April could drop into the low forties and high thirties. Yet the Island remained a comfortable sixty-five degrees.

As the couple headed past the Haus toward the springs, Silvano and Janessa continued down to the beach. "How do they manage to pass this place off as Maine? Does it ever snow here?"

"Apparently it did last year, over Rekkus's cabin. I heard Dana's moods affected the weather during her pregnancy. Sage informed me they are working on making the weather more believable." She slowed her pace. "Thank you."

"For what?"

"For...." *Choosing me over her*, she wanted to say but couldn't quite find the courage. "Understanding. I really didn't want anyone else on the beach tonight."

"Narsaria doesn't always appreciate people don't want company sometimes." He didn't elaborate. "Besides, she and my mother are going to get a massage and some mud bath facial."

"Sounds relaxing."

"Sounds messy. I don't mind getting messy for the right reasons."

"And what would the right reasons be?"

"You against the feeding wall." His voice washed over her in a near growl.

Her chest constricted as heat rushed through her. Wasn't it every woman's fantasy to be taken against the wall by her man? And it hadn't only lived up to the fantasy, it exceeded it. She didn't see him move from her side, but suddenly he stood before her. "I can smell your desire. You have no idea how hard it's been sitting next to you, watching you eat, listening to you talk, and knowing every para who passed by could smell my scent all over you. But I'm not going to take you now, I am going to abstain. We shall fast together, and, after your event, I will help you break your fast. Our lovemaking will make what happened today seem vanilla in comparison."

She gulped. Could she survive such a coupling? And then her heart sank. There would be no coming together for them tomorrow, and certainly not after. She would have memories and nothing else.

"Your despair radiates off you. What is it,

Nessa?" His voice, though low, held an air of impatience.

She would never get away with saying nothing. "Do you sense anyone nearby?"

He glanced at her, raising one regal black eyebrow then closed his eyes and breathed in the night air. After a moment, he opened them and shook his head. "There is no one."

"No one to hear."

"I can't guarantee Rekkus can't hear. I have heard rumors—"

"Rekkus knows the story," she blurted. "I need to tell you something distasteful about your friend Vlad."

"Did the tale come from Sarka?"

She nodded and could understand the disdain in his tone. "But it can be verified by Rekkus, apparently."

He almost dragged her to a nearby bench carved with a wolf's head on the outside of both armrests forcing her to sit. He stood over her, imposing but not intimidating. "Tell me."

"Where do I begin?" She took a deep breath and replayed her conversation with Sarka earlier, making sure to leave nothing out or to embellish anything either. When she finally refocused on him, his eyes glowed red. Sensing his anger was directed away from her, she reached for him. "I am sorry. I know he is a friend."

"He is a blight to my kind. Believe me, we will together deal with him upon our return and also make sure the story never sees the light of day." He lifted her from the bench. "Come, we must get to the cove so you can prepare. I want you to cleanse the bad energy from this distasteful situation and focus on what you need to deal with."

They strolled in silence along the path to the fire pit on the beach. The next day, a bonfire would be laid, logs from long-fallen trees piled high in an intricate pattern. She reached into her satchel and pulled out a moonflower, open under the moon's light. She caressed the silky petals, breathing in the seductive, heady perfume.

"My offer to burn, my desire to learn. With this flower, I offer my power." She laid the flower into the center of the pit beside four other offerings. A sage bundle, a pile of black sand, a lock of hair, and a glass of wine. Each had personal meaning for the witch who left it.

The rays of the moon called to her. She threw her head back and let the silver light wash over her. Her cells surged with the power of the upcoming super moon. Silvano brushed his knuckles down her neck. "You have no idea how temping you are, my little vixen."

"It is only the pull of the bond." She didn't move away, though.

"I thought so, too, but I am no longer as convinced."

She glanced at him. "What do mean?"

He strolled to the water's edge. The water came within inches of his feet but stopped as if Silvano could command it. "I wish I knew if this pull between us was more than a fated requirement. There are days I wish I had never met Narsaria. Days I wish you weren't a bond mate."

Her heart seized at those words.

"Do you ever wonder what would have happened

had we met and fate hadn't intervened?"

Every day. "We still would have had to deal with my paternal grandmother."

"I suppose she would have prevented a next step."

"Then there is my stepsister."

Silvano remained quiet, but she was unwilling to break the silence. Finally he spoke, his voice distant. "If not for this damned fated mess, perhaps we would have met and these feelings would have been so strong it could have overridden my hostilities toward your family. I can't believe that the overwhelming emotions running through me are what all bond mates experience."

"Perhaps you fight it too hard?" she murmured more to herself than to him.

He made a sound deep in his throat. "I have never been good at being told what I had to do."

He proved the lack time and again. Although he listened to his parents' advice, they knew telling him he had to do something offered a surefire way to ensure he did the opposite. He turned to her, his face passive. "I shouldn't have dropped this on you tonight. I'm being selfish. There is nothing either of us can do about our situation. But I want you to know I respect you, am in awe of your powers, and I do enjoy our time together."

For many women, those words would have been an insult along the lines of *but she has a great personality*, but he respected so few and wanted to be in the presence of fewer. So many things crossed her mind to say. But, in the end, she held her peace. It would do no good to tell him her plans. He might try and stop her or, worse, show some sign he approved of her decision and could then be with Narsaria.

"You are very quiet," he murmured.

"Was there something you needed me to respond to?"

He studied her until she squirmed. "No, I guess not."

At the sound of a man clearing his throat, she turned to find Rekkus leaning against the doorframe of his cottage. He sipped on the beer in his hand.

"Evening, Rekkus. We didn't disturb you I hope." Silvano nodded to the other man.

Shoving off the cottage, he shook his head. "No, but I didn't want you two discussing anything you didn't want me to hear."

Janessa added the word *else* to his sentence. He didn't want them discussing anything else—guaranteed he had heard an earful already. But he knew her plans already, so he knew of her marital problems, too. "We will head back to the Haus now so you can have some privacy."

"I doubt there will be much privacy in the cove tonight." He glanced at the fire pit. "By my count, there are eight more offerings to be made in the next couple of hours. Not everyone is as quiet as you two."

"The babies?"

"Sleep soundly, thankfully, but Dana doesn't. Her ear is always listening and every sound has her jumping out of bed. And they say I have super hearing." He gulped another swig from his bottle. "I would offer you both a beer, but I know Nessa is cleansing and you, Silvano, can't drink at all."

Silvano wrapped an arm around her and pulled her close. "I learned some ugly information about

Vlad tonight."

Janessa gaped at him. "Silvano."

"Rekkus and I know each other well. There is no need to preamble the situation or build to a question." He turned back to the tiger. "What kind of monster is hiding under Vlad's demeanor?"

Rekkus paused mid-gulp but showed no emotion or other response to Silvano's comment. Janessa knew the man too well. He replayed the scene in his head, thinking out every word he would eventually say. "I assume Sarka said something."

"Yes."

"I won't go into it, but I made a promise." He kept his promises. "But you can believe whatever you heard."

"So Sarka wouldn't have embellished."

"I doubt it would be possible." Rekkus's lips curled in disgust.

Silvano gave him a slight bow. "I see."

"I think you do." Rekkus placed the empty on the table. "All I ask is discretion."

"I promise you, not a whisper of what happened will be breathed into the air. I'll make sure Vlad understands he will need to take his long, eternal, worthless life and make amends somehow because he will no longer be welcome in our world."

"You are going to have him banished?" Shock ran through her. Nightwalkers had no greater humiliation.

"He can choose to take the sun, but he will no longer be welcome in our society."

The menace behind the words sent chills down her spine. She had never heard him speak with such absolute abhorrence.

Rekkus sneered. "Should he take a stroll in the morning light, please let me know so I can come witness it."

"Perhaps you could bring Sarka along."

"I believe she would find too much joy in his destruction for her own good." Rekkus cocked his head toward the open window. A second later, Janessa heard the unmistakable sound of a baby babbling. "If you will excuse me, my elder son appears to be ready to wake the house up. Hopefully, I can intercept him before he succeeds." Rekkus left them alone on the beach again.

Silvano turned toward the path back to the Haus. "You seem surprised by my stance on dealing with Vlad."

"He was a close friend and advisor."

"He hurt an innocent woman. She is your family, which means she is under my protection and his actions only more of an insult. And, before you say it, it doesn't matter this happened before we met."

"I hadn't thought of the timing, actually. Sage deserves justice, even if she doesn't know it." Janessa focused on the path that led up to the Haus. "May she never remember."

Silvano's arms wrapped around her waist. He pulled her close and kissed her hair. He offered her his silent, unrelenting support, something she had never been on the receiving end of before and leaving her more determined to continue on her path. Yet, as his fangs scraped her neck, she questioned her decisions all over again.

Chapter Five

The carpet below his feet would have become thread-worn had Silvano waited another hour to see Janessa. When he awoke at sunset, he found their room empty, with no sign of Nessa anywhere. He pushed down his hunger for her. He had fed before taking his rest at sunrise as she would be unable to feed him now. She needed her strength and, after a day's fast, would be too weak if she fed him and didn't feed herself. He shouldn't have been surprised not to find her at dinner. When he inquired, Myron explained she prepared for the evening, but Sage had let slip she had been working in the basement with Sarka on some secret project. Either way, his bride was avoiding him for whatever reason.

Tonight would be hard on her, and the need to support her and respect her choices had him pacing their room and not down in the lobby, demanding to see her. But the wall taunted him in a vicious cycle of memories which caused the boards to move, giving way to fantasies he never knew he had.

The wall clock read two thirty. Time to head

down to the beach. He placed the book on Rowan family history on the side table Myron had given him with a slight "To take your mind off other things." It hadn't. Every time he started to read, his mind wandered. He straightened his suit one last time before heading out. He opened his door to find his parents and Narsaria already in the hall.

"Janessa?" his mother inquired, looking around her son into the empty room.

"She is with her coven." He headed to the elevator. He didn't want to begin a discussion with any of them because what would he say? His emotions flew all over the place. Perhaps he fed off Janessa, but he didn't think so. And, for a man who didn't do emotions, these were raw and powerful. This whole week, the closer he felt to her, the more she slipped through his fingers. Yet, before this week, he had never cared.

The rest of the party must have sensed his lack of desire to converse because everyone, even Narsaria, remained quiet as they strolled down the path to the beach. As they crested the hill leading to the cove, they encountered four security guards, one human, two bears, and a wolf. In the distance, he could hear the howls of the young shifters locked in the barracks.

"You have your hands full tonight." Emil jerked his head in the direction from which the howls came.

"The full moon always brings out the craziness of the island." The human checked off their names. "Do you have any idea how crazy you have to be to top crazy?"

"You're human. I'm surprised Rekkus would leave the safety of the Rowans to a non-para." With the haughtiness of upper-crust para royalty bred deep into her, his mother showed her true colors.

"Right. Because it's the humans who are trying to hurt them." Kaleb tilted his head as if daring her to chew on that one. Silvano's mother had not been the first to underestimate the man. "But allow me to assure you while you noticed the shifters following you when you walked into the forbidden area behind the kennel last night, you never once paid heed to me."

"You followed us?"

"Exactly." He turned to Silvano and extended a hand in greeting. "Kaleb Theldon."

"The mermaid's husband."

"Proud owner of the title."

"You are a braver man than most." Silvano nodded in respect before excusing themselves. As they made their way down the hill, he said to his parents. "I wouldn't underestimate Kaleb, human or not. Anyone brave enough to mate with a Siren isn't one to balk at a set of fangs."

His mother huffed, but she didn't say anymore on the subject. How unlike her.

The large bonfire glowed bright, and a rock circle created around it seemed to hum. The Himalayan stones glowed with orange emphasized by the fire behind. Shifters in their animal forms surrounded the perimeter, providing tight security. And at least one gargoyle watched from the trees.

Dana smiled at them, offering a nervous little wave as they rounded her cabin. "Hello, Silvano."

"Dana." He reached out and ruffled the hair of the baby in her arms. "Rough night?"

"Same ole, same ole. This one here still isn't sleeping through the night." She dropped a kiss on his downy head.

"And, if this is the same baby, I understand he likes to wake everyone with him." He introduced her to his parents and Narsaria, who cooed appropriately. Rekkus, in tiger form, prowled around the fire before approaching the visitors. He came forward and sat beside his mate, his large feline head coming up to her shoulder. The baby screeched with joy and reached for his father a second before shifting into cub form tangled in a diaper and T-shirt.

"Are you kidding me?" Dana groaned in frustration as she placed the squirming cub on the ground. She wrestled the clothing off as the baby pounced at his father.

Rekkus growled, and the cub stopped. When he roared, the baby shifted back, sitting naked with a trembling lip. Rekkus moved to the boy, bowed his head, and purred as the baby reached up to tug his ears. Dana grabbed the baby and excused herself but not without glaring at her husband, rubbing at her temples. Rekkus turned back to the Dhampir guests before roaring in the direction of the precession coming toward them.

Silvano moved to sit with the handful of other guests. He scanned the water, sensing movement. A mermaid stuck her head up before diving under again. He took his seat on the fallen log as the coven came into view. The first three to approach the fire were staff members from the Haus. The yoga instructor, Myron the receptionist, and Dana took the place of the three fallen siblings. Five Rowan cousins who he knew only from pictures also joined the group around the fire. Next Cemil, Sage, and Cyrus, somber and more serious than he had ever seen. Finally,

Sarka and then Janessa.

"I have never seen Janessa or Sarka wear white." Narsaria marveled.

Neither had he, and she had never been more beautiful to his eyes. They had never had a real wedding, and now he wondered if she had wanted one. Perhaps they could rectify the omission here on the island, surrounded by the people who loved her. She kept her head lowered, but he could not take his eyes off her. With her dark hair plaited down her back, the long line of her neck, her creamy skin nearly glowed in the firelight.

"You've fallen in love with your mate."

Silvano rocked back in his seat. Narsaria spoke the truth. She might not have great magical powers like his Janessa, but she didn't need them with his emotions bursting from him. "I suppose I have."

He could see her struggle to swallow. "I should leave."

When she moved to stand, he placed a hand on her leg, staying her retreat. "You cannot, not yet. I can't allow you to disrupt the Rowans's ceremony."

"Of course. How selfish of me." She faced the witches, but he doubted she actually saw them.

"I am sorry I have hurt you." He regretted the pain he had inflicted all around. Mainly, he hated the hurt Janessa bore and, although guilt might have been easily divided between all four of them sitting here, he would bear the brunt of it on his broad shoulders, if they could all move on. "You must have sensed my distance over the last year. I admit my anger with the Fates for forcing my hand in mates. But I cannot say I am displeased now."

"Perhaps we have held onto our attachment out

of spite more than out of true emotion." She pulled at imaginary lint on her skirt. "I admit to being jealous of Janessa, but I have never borne her ill will. I had hoped the two of us could have taken our relationship to another level. And it stung to have it pulled out from under me by family, even through no fault of hers. I was also angry at myself for introducing you."

"If the Fates deemed us a couple, it would have happened whether you brought us into contact or not. Your involvement simply shortened the timeline."

With a heavy sigh, she slumped. "Perhaps you are right."

"You need to make amends to Janessa. We both do," Silvano conceded.

With the thirteen members of the coven surrounding the bonfire, Janessa started chanting. As she raised her hands, the flames grew higher, taking on a blue hue. The wind picked up, yet the fire never changed direction.

Suddenly, the coven threw their heads backs and lifted to the heavens a silent scream. Frozen in pain, Silvano stood, needing to make sure Janessa was okay.

A firm hand held him in place. "Keep your seat."

Silvano glanced over his shoulder to see the human, Kaleb. He hadn't sensed the man's presence and realized the genius of Rekkus hiring him for the Para Elite Forces. "She's in pain."

"They are communing with the others. Should you be concerned, follow Rekkus's lead. Both his mate and Cyrus are in the circle. If he is calm, you can be certain there is no danger." Kaleb went back to his patrol.

Janessa pushed the image of her bond mate in intimate conversation with Narsaria to the back of her mind. She must deal with the coven. They needed her and her abilities tonight. Lifting her arms to the heavens, she spoke words deeply ingrained within her psyche. The wind grew cold, and she gasped for breath.

The wind ceased to blow around her as she opened her eyes to stare into the great nothingness. All she had to do now was be patient and hope. Those murdered might have already crossed over, and they would choose who—if anyone—to come and talk to and who to ignore. The dead had the power when the veil reached this thinness. But there were three who passed and nine others in need of communication. The spirits tended to move through the easy ones first before dealing with the harder ones. She sent healing forces toward Cyrus, knowing his wait would be the longest and most difficult.

Although they could not see or communicate with one another or with anyone in the living realm while in this mystical state, they could sense each other. Cemil, whose empathic nature allowed him to feel what others experienced, would be wiped out by the end. If she felt a mere half of what he did, he suffered in empath overload.

The air shimmered and Saffron appeared before her, her blue eyes no less bright with death. Her blonde hair floated around her. "My sweet Janessa."

"Saffy." Janessa reached out, knowing she couldn't touch but needing to try. "Speak your words and know your peace."

"Love, continue to love, and know you are on the

right path."

"How can the two go hand in hand?" Tears blinded her vision.

"Only through pain can you find pleasure. Only through battle will you find peace. Love will come to you, my cousin, but you must trust your heart." Saffron turned as if being called.

"Be at peace, my cousin."

"Take care of Cyrus for us." She faded from view.

Her heart constricted, knowing the next two would be harder. Sandrine and Sarka had been the Dark Pair, and Celeste and Janessa the Fire Cousins, the four a force to be reckoned with and thick as thieves.

The shimmer and electrical spike. "Nessa, you fiery wench."

Janessa laughed in spite of herself. The icy-blue eyes held such love. "Sandy, speak your words and know your peace."

Sandrine cocked her head. "There is so much I wish to say, but not enough time. Know your heart, be true to it, and trust your soul. Take care of Cyrus. He is close to darkness."

"Be at peace, my cousin."

With a wink, the image faded.

Time stretched as she anticipated her last visit from the one she was closest to. The air sizzled, alerting her to the oncoming visit. "My beautiful Nessa."

Janessa open her eyes, wiping away tears she hadn't realized had started to flow. "Celeste, speak your words...and know your...peace."

"Do not shed tears for me or my sisters. Shed them for you. I feel your pain, know your trials, and you must follow through the breaking of the bond. Only then will you be free."

"I thought...."

"You must follow this through. You must. There is no going back. I can say no more."

"Are you going to ask me to take care of Cyrus?"

"No, because you will need all your strength to take care of yourself. Be at peace, my sister cousin." Celeste reached out to her.

"Those are my words to you."

"I know." She smirked, blowing her a kiss. "Be well, be one with the goddess and with yourself."

"I miss you."

"I have to go and need you to allow me to leave."

Tears racked her. "Be at...peace, Celeste. Know you are loved."

Then the nothingness returned, leaving Janessa alone and weighted with survivor guilt and yet a sense of peace she hadn't known since the murders. She felt first Saffron pass over then Celeste, and finally Sandrine. The light of the fire came into view, and Janessa, finally able to move, lowered her head and took in each of the coven around the fire, pausing only on Cyrus who paled and might collapse any second. In a loud voice she chanted, "Be at peace, our sisters. Move from this world and may we see you on the other side. By the goddess, we are whole again."

Cyrus gripped his head and cried out in pain. The streak of black fur shot past her before any of the coven could reach for him. As Cyrus crumpled toward the ground, Rekkus shifted from tiger to human, naked in the firelight. He lifted Cyrus in his arms. Only Dana dared to step forward. But the three other siblings, at a distance, followed them into their cabin,

Sarka supporting Cemil as they moved into the privacy they desperately needed.

Silvano reached for her and pulled her into his arms. She knew she should push him away, but, weak and drained, she needed his support. "Will Cyrus be all right?"

She nodded into his chest. "Eventually, but he will need time to come to terms with what he heard. This was harder on him than anyone else."

"Carrying guilt weighs a man down."

"It does. He'll stay with Rekkus tonight and until he can face anyone else."

"Why with Rekkus?" The voice of her mother-in-law came from behind her.

"The cabin is the only place he can be without gloves. He is safe there and they understand him. The siblings decided days ago Cyrus would move in with Rekkus and his family during his healing. Each must come to terms with what they learned."

"What were they told?" Emil asked.

"I have no idea. Each message is special to each person."

"And your message?" Silvano ran a hand over her hair.

"To trust my path and take care of Cyrus."

"I think for tonight Cyrus is well taken care of. Perhaps you will allow me to take care of you."

She nodded, exhaustion weighing heavy on her. He wrapped an arm around her waist as they made their way off the beach, pausing only long enough to glance in the open window to see Dana holding Cyrus on the sofa as Rekkus crouched before his friend. Cyrus rested within the embrace of friends. "What is the state of their relationship?"

"Monogamous, though we all thought the Fates would have them sharing a mate. One day his mate will come."

"When he least expects it." Silvano lightened the mood with a chuckle.

"Cousin," Orion and Willow called from behind.

Silvano insisted his parents go ahead without them and kept a supportive arm around Janessa as they turned back to the cove and the three people seeking her attention. "Are you up for this?"

She nodded and plastered a smile she didn't feel in greeting. Janessa loved her family, but she'd worked much of the day in Sarka's workroom to break the curse on the knife and items brought onto the island by others meaning to do harm to her cousins, and the mental toll of the evening removed the remaining bit of energy left. "Orion and Willow, you cut it close tonight."

"It couldn't be helped." Willow wiped a weary hand over her eyes. "We were working to find a lost child with time not on our side."

"Oh no, please tell me you succeeded."

"Thankfully, yes." Orion, too, showed exhaustion, his usually lively eyes dulled with weariness.

"Will you be leaving in the morning, or are you extending your stay?"

Willow stared at her foot as she kicked a pebble. "I think I will stay another week."

"Myron suspected you might." Willow had been dealing with her grief in her own ways, and a few weeks on the island had made a difference. The massacre of the siblings had not only broken the family but the coven as well. Until tonight, the group had been unable to function as a team. "And you, Orion?"

"That, I suppose has to do with whether I am needed here or not." His knowing glance bespoke he knew more or perhaps suspected more about her situation. He turned to her bond mate who stood quietly at her side, his arm around her waist. "You must be Silvano."

"It's a pleasure to meet more of Janessa's family." He first greeted Orion and then Willow followed by Raine, the youngest of the Rowan cousins. "So your fathers were all siblings?"

"No," Willow answered. "It is the custom within the Rowan family for the men to take the name of Rowan from the women."

"Most are only too happy to do so," Raine put in.

Janessa turn to her man. "Within the Wiccan community, the Rowan name is both respected and revered, and the Rowan witches are powerful."

"I know a bit about the power of the Rowans." She couldn't tell if he was being sarcastic or not. "Will you excuse us? Janessa is about to collapse where she stands, and I want to get her something to eat and perhaps to bed."

"You are breaking your fast? I thought—"

"No, I will continue my fast through sunrise." Janessa interrupted her young cousin before she could say more. She could not allow her husband to discover her plans before she could go through with them. Those on the island who knew hadn't told anyone else. But the summoning very well could have let this be known. Much like two of the cousins had pleaded with her to take care of Cyrus, it could be assumed any or all of the three had requested the same for her.

They exchanged good-byes and, with a strong arm wrapped around her waist, Silvano moved out of sight before lifting her into his arms and carrying her at vampire speed toward the Haus. "Do you want me to take you straight to our room or through the lobby?"

Laying her head against his shoulder, she mumbled, "No lobby please." She didn't have the energy to deal with anyone, and she could see his family through the open lobby doors. They would need to be social if they saw her and Silvano. She hadn't eaten since before sunrise, hadn't slept in days. And, although she'd finished two of the three things she had to get done, the hardest remained.

He leapt from the ground to their balcony as if jumping the curb. After entering through the open double doors, he laid her gently on the bed. "I had hoped to have you eat, but it appears to be not an option. Can I get you some wine or something to drink?"

"Water would be nice." Wine would have been perfect, but she needed a clear head and fortitude to get through the night. "You may feed if you need to."

"No, if you can fast, so can I."

Janessa sent a thankful prayer up to the goddess. If he didn't feed, breaking the bond would be easier. He handed her a glass of water before lying next to her. Once she took a sip, he pulled her into his protective embrace. They lay there for what seemed like an hour before he finally spoke.

"We need to have a serious talk. But I fear tonight is not the right time and maybe the island not the right place."

"Perhaps." Deep inside, her conscience screamed, *Speak your mind because you will never get a chance to say anything else.* Her lids grew heavy. "I must rest. Do not feel the need to stay if you would rather be with your family."

"You are also my family, Janessa, and, at the moment, I sense you need me more." He brushed the hair off her forehead and allowed her to fade into blissful and exhausted sleep.

She awoke half an hour later to a sharp knock at the door. Panic filled her. What if the sun had risen?

Silvano, still awake but showing the signs of the sun's pull, released his arm to allow her to get up. He was weakened by not feeding, and, as the moon began to set, his need to sleep grew. "Do you want me to get the door?"

She was touched. As heavy as his limbs must be this close to sunrise, he still offered. She gulped, unable to talk over the lump in her throat. She shook her head. Easing out of bed, she crept over and opened the door enough to see who was there but not to allow those on either side of the door to see one another. Sarka, Maya, Raine, and Cemil stood in a solemn row.

"It's time." Cemil grasped her hand. "We will be here. Should you need us, simply yell out."

She nodded and closed the door again. No one knew if she would have time to get to her new room before the heartbreak turned to desolation. Those she had spoken to differed in their opinion. From a few hours to less than sixty minutes. Either way, her pain would come too soon.

Silvano appeared so peaceful in the bed. She knew he hadn't entered "the sleep." He breathed yet at ever-growing intervals, and his arm lay across his eyes. She came to the side of the bed, lifted his hand, and placed it on her heart. He opened his eyes and smiled.

"Who was at the door?"

"Some of my cousins."

Step three. You must be alone and looking into your mate's eyes. They must hear you speak your words and allow you to walk away. The pain will grow progressively worse over the hours. If the couple feels they have made a mistake, the bond can be mended within the first two hours, without consequence. In the case of blood feeders, once they have fed from another, there is no turning back. When you break the bond predetermined by the Fates, you risk losing your powers.

"You need to eat."

"I will."

He pulled her hand to his lips. "Good. You will need your strength."

"I love you, Silvano." She traced his full lips one last time. "Always will."

Before the sleep took him, she laid his heavy hand on his stomach. "Nessa?"

"I release you." She stepped back, watching the horror fill his face, and he took a deep breath, preparing to yell, but "the sleep" came over him.

Her body starting shaking, and the next thing she knew Cemil escorted her from the room in a supportive embrace. She didn't remember yelling out or calling for help, but perhaps she did, or maybe Cemil took her emotional distress as a scream for help.

"Keep breathing."

In the hall, Sarka silently offered her a silken bundle which she knew held the Knife of Moshchnost. No words were needed. It was time to finish breaking this curse, and it could only be done with the descendant of the curser freely handing the items back. There had been more to it—hours spent clearing every gem and engraving of the dark magic and finally cleansing the blade with her own blood. Being a curse breaker had never been an easy talent to have.

"Do you want me to go in with you?" Cemil reached up and brushed down her hair.

"Would you?"

"Of course. How long will Emil remain awake?"

"Livia can only stay awake ten minutes after sunrise, so she should be down for the day. This time of year, he should maintain a wakeful state for a little over an hour." As she came to the room at the end of the hall, she closed her eyes finding her center and the strength she needed to continue. This part should be simple, but she'd learned nothing in her life went to plan.

She scratched on the door, as her father-in-law had hearing rivaling Rekkus's. When Emil opened the door, he glanced between Cemil and Janessa, concern marring his usually stoic face.

"May we come in?"

"Of course. What can I do for you both?"

"I'm here to return something belonging to you." She reached for his hand and placed the bundle in his palm. "It is long overdue, but only here on the island did I have the last of the items I needed to complete the task."

"What is this?" His fingers hesitated as he untied

the ribbon. When he went to drop the knife, Janessa wrapped his fingers around it. "Is this a joke? You know I cannot touch this."

"The curse is broken. Please trust me. All I want to do is give you back your birthright."

Hesitant, Emil reached for the knife, but as soon his fingers brushed the gold handle, his grip tightened and he pulled the dagger from the fabric, lifting it into the candlelight. Power sizzled around the man. "I have dreamed of this day. I was so young when the curse took our birthright from us. I forgot its power."

"We must go, Janessa." Cemil nudged, squeezing her arm.

"We have misjudged you, Janessa. My bride and I have a lot to make up for." His eyes never lifted from the knife as he turned it in the light.

She shook her head. "The knife shouldn't have been cursed in the beginning. When you return to your home, you will find a selection of other items I have successfully removed the evil from. I had hoped to get to them all, but this"—she indicated the knife—"took preference. Perhaps you can find someone to take care of the rest. You won't need a great curse breaker but someone who has some knowledge. I have left instructions as to which are still cursed and what is needed to clear them. Those I couldn't get to have moon phases that won't show for another year, some two."

"With this, there is no rush. You will have plenty of time." He noticed her flinch. "What aren't you saying?"

Janessa blindly reached for the door. She had to leave; she didn't want this confrontation, couldn't handle it. "Please take care of Silvano." She opened the door and stepped out, knowing the first rays of sun would be touching the red wool threads of the carpets covering the second floor hallway.

"Sleep well, Emil." Cemil closed the door behind them.

Janessa couldn't speak as she concentrated on trying to breathe with lungs that now hurt to expand. If anyone spoke, she couldn't hear it over the ringing in her ears. She had to get out of the building. The walls were closing around her. Only with the gentle prodding of Cemil and the strength of his arms did she make it into the elevator, but, by the time the door opened on the first floor, pain tore through her like nothing she had ever experienced. Her very soul ripped from her, stitch by meticulous stitch.

She reached for Cemil, needing his support, only to find him buckled over in pain. Maya wrapped an arm around her waist while placing her palm on Janessa's forehead. Over the roar in her ears, she couldn't hear what she chanted but she did hear Myron yell, "Rekkus, we need you."

Seconds later, the Earth spun, her feet left the floor, and her head lay against the heat of the were-tiger. Maya's touch never left her. "I have you, Nessa."

The sun blinded her as they exited the confines of the Haus. "Cemil?"

"He was unprepared for your agony. He will be fine. He needs a few minutes to get on top of the pain."

She heard nothing more as the soul-wrenching torment escalated and thankful darkness washed over her.

Silvano fought through the sleep. Moments before the moon rose, he shot out of bed. Fury burned him like the sun's rays. What the hell had his bride done? He tried to work past his hunger. His need to feed had never been so strong. He paced the room, waiting for the sun to drop. Pausing at the closet, he threw it open, knowing what he would encounter. Empty hangers hung alongside those holding his clothes. He turned, seeing red, and ripped the drawers from the dresser, every one of them empty.

A drawer hit the wall with such force it splintered, leaving a hole in the plaster. She had left. He couldn't sense her presence, but he couldn't sense anything over the growing need to feed. As the last vestiges of sunlight fell over the horizon, he threw open the door to find out if Janessa had gone through the portal. He would find her if he had to track her all over this planet.

Four stood before him on his threshold. "Get out of my way."

"Not so quick." The tall man, who resembled Cyrus, stood before Silvano, not budging.

"Where is Janessa?"

"I don't know."

"Aren't you Orion, the great tracker?"

"I am."

"So you could track her."

"If I wanted to, but I have no reason to track her for you. She left you, Silvano, and I plan to make sure her wishes are respected." Orion stepped to the side and indicated a small brunette.

"Rekkus sent a message. Your presence is not

required in the mess hall tonight." Chad, one of the security guards who'd worked for Rekkus for years, a bear shifter, urged the lady toward Silvano. "Your dinner is served."

"Not interested."

"Not an option," Chad stated. "Rekkus says it's this or nothing."

"It's Janessa or nothing."

"Son, what is going on?" Emil strolled down the hall toward them. "Where is Janessa?"

"That is what I want to know." Silvano's thinly wrapped temper snapped, and he put his fist through the wall. "Get her out of here."

Chad nodded to the fourth man, another security guard. "Max, get her off this floor and inform Rekkus it's plan B."

"What the hell is plan B?" Silvano demanded.

Chad shrugged. "No idea, but it's not my problem."

Silvano made his way to the elevator, waiting only long enough for the feeder to leave the floor; he didn't trust himself in the enclosed lift. All it would have taken was her to prick her finger and his animal craving would come out. Although he was hungry and tempted, his heart wanted nothing but Janessa, and if this was how he had to prove it to her, he would. "Janessa left me."

"How can she leave?" His father's voice remained calm.

"She's a curse breaker," he growled.

"But your bonding isn't a curse." His mother spoke from behind him. So caught up in his agony, he'd never heard her approach.

"Really? You have both treated it like a curse

since the moment you met her. You have made her the focus of your disdain and hostility for five years. Why wouldn't she treat our bonding as a curse? And I haven't given her any reason to believe I felt differently. It is my burden to bear."

"She came to see me at sunrise this morning." His father reached into his long coat to hand his son the sheathed knife from within. "She returned our people to us."

So he now knew what she had been working on all week.

"Selfless." His mother caressed the gem hilt. "We owe her more than a simple apology. You must find her. We must make this right."

Silvano let his fingers run over the gems of a knife he had only stared at through glass. "How?"

"I suspect the knife in my office is a fake she had created so she could work on the real one. It isn't like anyone would have given her the item."

"It was a risky and brave move on her part."

Silvano handed the object back to his father. "An act of love."

His father and mother didn't follow him into the elevator. He ignored the people in the lobby and didn't bother asking Myron where to find Janessa. The Rowans, both family and staff, had rallied around her and wouldn't help him. He made his way to the dining room, knowing she wasn't there, but he had to check anyway.

A strong hand on his shoulder stopped him. "I told you not to come in here tonight."

"I have to find my mate, bear. Do not stand in my way."

"Normally I wouldn't, but she isn't your mate

anymore."

Silvano went to swing at the shifter, but the bear whose strength matched Rekkus's stopped the fist and held it. "Don't make me call the boss. It won't end well for you. She is not in there."

"But she is on the island?"

The bear relaxed and took pity on him. "No one left through the portal today."

He exhaled in relief. "Thank you."

"Don't thank me yet."

Silvano marched into the night and breathed in deep, rich scents. All sense of Janessa ended in the lobby. She must have been carried. The pain she must have felt nearly brought him to his knees. But she wouldn't be alone, so he honed in on the life-force of the most Rowans in one place. One down on the beach. Three in the Haus. The rest were in the forest in the center of the island. In the trees. He ran full speed as if the devil rode on his heels, and perhaps he did.

He made the large jump onto the deck of the tree house and, peeking through the partially open doorway, saw Janessa curled into the fetal position on the bed, her hair soaked with sweat. Silvano ran to get to her, to hold her, to make this all better. As he reached for the door, he hit an invisible wall preventing him from entering, and the force of his advance equaled the amount of him being thrown back. Stalking back to the open door, he begged, "Nessa, baby, let me in."

She didn't answer, didn't seem to even hear him, so he raised his voice. "Nessa, allow me admittance."

"Not on your life, bloodsucker." Sarka came into view, throwing the door wide. The desk was covered in books, some he recognized as his bride's strewn around the room open as if Sarka were reading them all.

"How did I know you wouldn't be far?" he snarled. "Let me help her."

Sarka stood inches from him, yet, for all his ability to get to her, she might have been miles away. "She did this to get away from you. Why would I let you near her again?"

Silvano's roar of anger shook the tree. And he turned, holding onto the railing until it splintered under his grip.

"Silvano," Rekkus warned from the corner of the deck. He leaned against the tree house as casually as if about to discuss the weather. Rekkus turned and groaned long before footsteps could be heard on the steps below. "Cyrus, what are you doing here?"

"I wanted to see how Janessa fared. What the fuck is he doing here?" Cyrus demanded, anger in his voice. He took a step toward Silvano but Rekkus stopped him, hooked the repair worker's safety rope to his belt, and returned to his place on the wall. "What the hell, Rek?"

"It's a long drop, and he is angry. Just doing my job."

Cyrus took in the broken rail then seemed to judge the distance to the ground and the length of the rope. "What about you?"

"Me?"

"What if he throws you over the edge?"

Rekkus gave Cyrus a droll look, probably because he knew it never would have even entered Silvano's brain, angry or not, to try and fight the tiger with physical strength. "I would land on my feet, if he were so disposed to even try and take that route."

The two men seemed locked in a stare down, before Cyrus cursed under his breath and turned back to Silvano. "So what are you doing here? Janessa released you. You can now flap your batty wings over the horizon with the wicked stepsister."

"I hate damned stereotypes."

"If the wings fit," Sarka sniped from inside.

"We are not all the same. I am not Vlad, and I cannot turn into a bat."

"You are all the same. I can smell your hunger, your need." Sarka placed her silver nail ring to her neck and pressed until blood trickled. "Feed on me, then."

"No." He stepped back.

She stepped forward, over the threshold. "Feed, vamp."

He pushed her back, his mouth watering with hunger. The red richness of her blood assailed his nostrils. "No!"

"Sarka, step back," Rekkus demanded. Something in his voice had her retreating back to the safety of the dwelling.

"Janessa!" Silvano pounded both sides of the doorframe in frustration, splintering the outer frame before finally turning on Rekkus. "What if it were your mate?"

He didn't see the tiger move, but, a second later, he was a hairsbreadth away. "Don't compare me to you. The difference between my kind and yours is my mate has never been in doubt of how I felt. My whole being is in making her understand she is the very center of my world. Without her, I am nothing. She never goes a day without knowing my heart beats for her, with hers. And she would never have reason to break our bond."

"I need to prove to her exactly that. I need her to know I love her." The words exploded from him before he could stop them. But once he uttered them, he realized they didn't make him weak, but his love for her gave him strength he'd never understood.

Rekkus stepped back, assessed him, and cocked his head. "Sarka, let him in."

"What?" she screeched in disbelief.

"He speaks the truth. He loves her." Cemil stood, pale and unstable. "Let him enter."

"Are you going to attach a safety rope to Cemil?" Cyrus demanded.

"He isn't going to piss anyone off." Rekkus repeated, "Let him enter."

"Fine, but I am not leaving them alone."

"Suit yourself." Silvano focused on Janessa's form on the bed.

"You may enter."

No sooner than the words were spoken he darted to her side and gathered her in his arms.

"She stays here, within this room," Rekkus announced. "You being with her is contingent on remaining within the confines of these four walls, and if Nessa says leave, you're gone. Do you understand?"

"Yes." He held her close, wanting to feed but knowing he couldn't. She was weak, and his needs must come second.

Janessa arched in pain, trying to push him away. "No."

Pulling her closer, he brushed his lips into her hair. "Nessa, I love you. Please come back to me."

She shook her head and moaned before lapsing

back into unconsciousness. Silvano lifted her body and adjusted them both on the bed. Holding her tight, he infused her with his strength, all the while doing his best to ignore the angry nails tapping on the table in the corner.

"I will be within earshot, Sarka, should you need me," Rekkus announced.

"Because earshot for you is anywhere on the frecking island, really," Cyrus snapped in a chipped voice what Silvano had been thinking.

Silvano could hear their footsteps receding down the ramp. He knew Rekkus could, should he choose, still hear them long after they could hear him, but it didn't matter what he heard because obviously everyone on the island had been in on his bride's plans. The one person he knew might hold the key to win Janessa back was the one person least likely to help.

Glancing up and catching him staring at her, Sarka demanded, "What?"

"How do I fix this?"

"Like I would help you." She dragged her nails across the table in disdain.

"How about you help her?" He refused to break eye contact. "She told me about what happened with Vlad, and I promise I will be dealing with him when I return home. I understand why you don't trust my kind."

"You understand nothing. How can you?" She stood, her chair falling backward. "Your kind feeds without thought."

"I cannot help what I was born to be. This is the only way I can survive."

Sarka made a sound of disgust, going to the

window.

"Just as you and your siblings are different, we aren't all the same. I need you to help me save her." He would beg this witch if he had to.

He thought she wouldn't say anything until, in a voice quiet and full of concession, she offered, "You can't feed."

"Done." He would go as long as necessary if it would bring Janessa back to him.

She looked at him, making sure he understood the gravity of her words. "If you feed from anyone but her, the bond will be forever broken. There is.... Never mind."

"What aren't you telling me?"

"She might have traded her powers in exchange for your freedom." Sarka's anger sang out through every syllable. "Will you love her if she is mundane?"

"I could have walked away tonight. I could have fed after fasting. But I am here. I'll be right at her side no matter what happens." Janessa shivered in his arms, and Sarka brought a blanket and threw it over them both.

"This doesn't mean anything, bloodsucker."

He didn't respond, as her comment lacked bite.

Sarka returned to her corner, restored the chair to its upright position, and took her seat. She focused on the book open on the table, flipping furiously through the pages, pausing every so often to chant something then cursing when it seemed to have no effect on Janessa's state of being. "Damn it, Nessa. I am not a curse breaker."

Long after his arms went numb and his need to feed nearly consumed him, the sun rose, taking him into the sleep of his people, but for once it wasn't restful. He fought the darkness, remaining alert to her heartbeat and the sounds around them. Concern Sarka could open a door or window, leaving him completely vulnerable to the sun's beams, kept him from full rest..

Yet, when the sun set, he found Sarka collapsed over her book. She didn't even wake when Sage came by with some soup for Janessa and a plate for her sister. Although they tried, they got no more than a spoonful or two into Janessa. "Why doesn't she wake?"

"I don't know." Sage brushed a tear away. "I work in herbs; this is not something I can fix with plants. I can only hope to help keep her strength up until she can fight this herself."

"Can none of you help her?"

"We are trying. We have everyone checking every book in the library."

"And my mother has someone searching Janessa's private library at the house." Silvano would have laughed at the disbelief in the sibling's faces had he not been so damned worried. "Someone Janessa trusts."

"All we can do is wait and hope." Sage took a seat next to the bed and started wrapping some sage smudge sticks.

Over the next twenty-four hours nothing changed. Maya came, chanted, and forced some of Sage's teas down her. Silvano's need to feed grew by the minute. He had never been this long without feeding, and he worried he couldn't hold out the seventy-two hours Sarka and Sage believed he needed to wait to bring her back, and even then they weren't sure it would work. They were working under assumptions and tapping into myths, rather than spells they knew. He refused to even think she might not be able to come back. The only Rowan who hadn't been through the room at this point was Cyrus who, since the confrontation on the deck with Rekkus, remained absent.

But he focused on the lack of response from Janessa as she lay in his arms. He spoke to her of things he wanted for them. Children, their own home, and more time with her family. How his parents wanted to make amends. Even her stepsister had come at the urging of Cemil. To explain there was nothing between Silvano and herself. But all in vain as Janessa seemed unaware anyone was there. When she opened her eyes, they were vacant.

"You need to feed," Sarka barked from the door.

"No." He closed his eyes against the wave of hunger those words drove into him. If she cut open a vein, he feared he would leap on her.

"You need to feed from Janessa." Myron appeared from behind the other woman. She walked around Sarka and placed her cards down on the foot of the bed.

"I thought we had to hold off seventy-two hours."

"Neither of you will make it." Myron laid the cards down again, and the same four cards appeared. "Now, you can't wait."

Myron pulled Sarka with her as she exited. Maya followed, closing the door, leaving them for the first time alone in the tree house. With shaking hands, he lifted her hair from her neck. The pulse drew him. He knew her heartbeat, could taste it on his tongue. Leaning back against the wooden headboard, he controlled his breathing. Once be believed he could master his hunger, he pulled her against his chest.

"Do it," Sarka hissed through the door.

Running his tongue over his fangs, he leaned into her neck and let his teeth pierce her porcelain flesh. Immediately, the rich liquid rushed, and he drank. He drank until his strength returned. When a hand gripped his knee and she arched into him, he drank some more. As she gasped, she began to come alive. He could feel the power rushing through her, could feel her powers returning. Then the warm glow of life in her filled him as sharp, stabbing pains assaulted his chest like a thousand pins. He sensed their bond repairing. He pulled away as she cried out in pain.

They sat staring at each other, her head lying on his shoulder, neither speaking nor moving, as if stuck in a private tableau.

"Why?" She cleared her throat, her voice rough from lack of use.

He eased himself out from behind her, kissing her shoulder before he got up. After pouring a cup of Sage's tea, he brought it to her and helped her bring it to her lips. "Are you hungry?"

She shook her head, as her eyes closed like someone who hadn't slept in days and perhaps she hadn't. She had been lost to him and herself. Only time would tell if she was willing to come back. He crossed to the door and opened it wide so the women outside could see her. "She is resting, and, though not hungry, she will be when she awakes."

"I'll have something brought up immediately." Myron raced down the stairs.

"You have seen her. Now we need some time alone." Silvano hid his shock when Sarka did no more than nod and follow Myron down the steps, though at a slower pace.

"I'll be out here if she or you need me." Maya offered a kind word.

"Thank you." Silvano left the door ajar as they would be bringing food shortly, and it would ease Maya's mind. He had come to respect and admire the youngest of the Rowans. Her healing abilities might not be as strong as Sage's, but she had only come into her power when the killing happened. He sat on the mattress beside his love, grabbing her hand and bringing the inside of her wrist to his lips. "Do not ever leave me, Nessa."

"I don't understand why are you here and not with Narsaria?" Janessa's voice, heavy with exhaustion, came out soft and small.

"I don't want your stepsister. It has been a long time since I have."

"But I saw you on the beach. You two were touching and—"

He placed a finger to her lips. "I prevented her from leaving and disrupting your ceremony. She figured out something I had yet to admit to myself."

"What?" The wide-eyed disbelief was something he hoped to never see again.

"She saw I had fallen in love with my bride."

Her breath hitched, and tears filled her eyes. "Don't say it if you don't mean it."

"Janessa, look at me. Look in me. If your love can break what the Fates decreed, why is it unbelievable my love would bring us back?" He eased in behind her so he could hold her close again. "How could you doubt, even without words, my feelings? I thought the last few days we had been closer than ever."

"I did doubt then I saw you both. And my cousins who came through during the summoning convinced me I had to go through with my plans to be fully happy."

Silvano moaned. "I will never forgive myself for the pain you had to go through for me to prove my love."

She buried her head into his chest. "I lost hope I could make you happy."

"You cannot lose what I never gave you. I took out my frustration at the Fates on you. Your grandmother's taking so much from my family didn't help matters. Yet you gave it all back. Everything. And asked nothing in return. I don't deserve you or your love. But I will spend the rest of our very long life working to prove to you I can earn it and will be the sort of man you deserve."

"I don't know what to say."

"You don't have to say anything yet. Simply know you are loved."

They remained silent until after she had eaten half a medium-rare steak and kale salad. "Why didn't you feed?"

"I was tempted more than you can know. But I knew if I did, we would be over."

"How could you have known?"

"I knew it here." He tapped his chest. "You are the other part of me, Janessa, and I might have been slow in figuring it out, but now I know the only thing that will separate us is death."

Tears flowed, and he pulled her into his arms. "I'm sorry I am so weepy."

"Don't apologize for feeling."

They cuddled in each other's arms, in peaceful silence. As the sun started to dawn, he lay on the bed and breathed a sigh when she curled up next to him. They still had a lot to work through, and he had more to make up for, but now they were where they needed to be. Together.

Chapter Six

Janessa stretched before opening her eyes. Her body ached like she'd spent a week bedridden with the flu, and she remembered what had happened. Fear racked her. What if it had all been a dream, and Silvano hadn't come? Yet her heart didn't hurt, and hope flared.

"You going to open those beautiful eyes or continue to pretend to be asleep?" Silvano asked, humor lacing his deep voice.

Turning her head on the pillow, she opened her eyes. Her bond mate placed a tray on the side table and sat on the edge of the bed. "What time is it?"

"Two hours past sunset."

"Why didn't you wake me?" She scooted up the bed to lean against the headboard. He laid the silver tray on her lap, removed the cover, and delicious aromas filled her senses.

"You needed to rest. Now you need to eat."

"Do you need to feed first?"

He shook his head. "No, I drank some at dinner."

The fork stopped in midair as her body froze. Silvano never drank from someone else and the thought of him partaking of someone's essence shocked her as well as sent a full amount of jealousy through her. "You did?"

"At Sarka's behest. You are too weak for me to feed, and she wanted me to be strong for you."

"So you fed from...."

"A glass."

The sense of relief hearing he hadn't fed from another was greater than it should have been. "Oh."

"It was a man's blood."

"Oh." She giggled and took a large bite.

"It was awful." He scrunched his nose like a child forced to eat Brussels sprouts.

"Do men taste different than women?" The thought had never occurred to her before.

"Yes, and although some may prefer the gamey taste of male blood, my preference lies along the sweeter side. Each to his own, I guess. But, from a glass, it's cold and thick and, well...not you."

"Good." The savory steak nearly melted in her mouth. Life did seem to be getting better every moment. "So, how long do you have to stay away from me?"

"According to Sarka or Myron?"

"Myron. Sarka might not be the most reliable."

"Two more nights."

He sounded so put out a giggle bubbled up from within her.

"Keep laughing."

"Oh, come here."

"No."

"No?"

He stalked to the other side of room. "I can't trust myself not to feed."

"You just drank."

"It's not the same."

"You went nearly three long days without feeding."

"Because I thought I would lose you. The first day was because you were fasting and needed strength for the summoning. The next two were to save us. Without fear, my self-control is at a low point." He ran fingers through his almost perfect hair, its disheveled appearance adding to how out of control he must feel. "You scared me like nothing I have ever felt. Here I finally realized what you meant to me and you were pulling away. I could feel it, but I never thought you had a way to break the bond. But leave it to my curse breaker to find the out clause."

"I never considered being with you a curse."

"And neither did I." He spoke with such conviction, she believed him.

"Tell me."

He opened the shuttered window, taking in the smells of the night. "When I woke the other morning, I knew you were gone, and I felt dead inside. No, when you released me, I felt dead and helpless. The sleep overcame me, and I have never fought it so hard. I even managed to come awake before the sun set. Little good it did me, as I couldn't leave the room."

"I am sorry."

"Don't. Don't ever be sorry for doing the only thing you thought you could. Rekkus gave me a big dose of shame."

Oh good lawd! Rekkus took his job as protector of all Rowans very seriously. "I'm afraid to ask."

"He told me in so many words, had I treated you

like my princess, you never would have wanted to go free."

She didn't think she could cry anymore, but tears filled her eyes. She wiped at the pools with the back of her hand, not wanting them to fall. "I never wanted to be a princess."

"But you are." He gripped the windowsill as if it would prevent him from coming to her. He must have sensed she was close to losing it all over again. "I was angry, I felt trapped, and you presented an easy target. But what did you give me? Nothing but love and affection. Little by little, I grew to enjoy our time together, but did I give an inch? No. I let you think you didn't matter, made you believe I preferred your sister over you."

"But I understood. You cared for Narsaria first, and had I not come to the party at your house those many years ago, you and she might have married."

"Oh, and that would have been perfect. Because you and I would have met on my wedding day and discovered we were mates. And Narsaria and I were not heading to marriage. I didn't feel for her anything like I feel for you."

"It's the nature of bonding."

"No. I have done some research on my own over the last few nights while you slept. Everything says, when a loveless bond is broken, the inability to feed on and be with others would dissolve immediately. The freedom would be instant."

"And?"

"They threw a woman at me. My favorite type, even, and I didn't want her. I wanted you. I needed to make sure you were okay." This time he did cross the room and cup her face, forcing her to meet his gaze.

"Why? Because I love you. Because, deep inside, I know the Fates were right. You are my bond mate and, once you are stronger, I want to complete the bonding."

She blinked. Then blinked again because through all of this, the last thing—actually not even the last thing—she ever imagined would be that he would want to take their bonding to the final level. To do so they would connect their life-forces. They would be able to communicate without words, and they would live together and die together.

"There is more." He got down on one knee and opened his palm to reveal a large diamond ring. "Will you marry me? Will you pledge your love before your friends and family?"

She couldn't breathe as she stared between the ring, gaudy as it might be, and Silvano who knelt breathless with anticipation.

"Good lord, say yes already," Sarka bemoaned from the open window. "I came to see if you were all right. I didn't think I would have to witness this cavity-inducing scene."

"Sarka." Silvano's voice held a frustration he didn't hide.

"Sarka, please go away." Janessa loved her cousin but really wished to have this moment without anyone but her and her man.

"Oh right. I'll be outside when you are done."

"Sarka."

"Fine. I will be at the Haus when you are done."

"Thank you."

In the distance, she heard something sounding like, "Whatever."

"That went about as well as everything else in

our relationship," Silvano groaned, but his voice held lightness. "So, again, will you marry me?"

"We are bonded. You want to complete the full bonding. There is really no reason to marry me under the moon."

"As a little girl, did you dream of marrying beneath your beloved Luna?"

"Well, yes."

"Wearing a white dress, surrounded by those who love you?"

"Of course, but...."

"So let me make your dream come true."

"Yes." She threw her arms around him, taking him off guard so they landed in a mess of arms and legs on the wood floor. When she lifted her head, she found him staring up at her, heat and hunger in his eyes. "Oh."

"I should take a hike and cool down." Despite the sentiment, he made no move to get up.

"You should."

"Myron said to put your needs first."

"Don't forget Sarka."

"Who could forget Sarka?" He lifted his head to take her lips. "Oh, hell with it."

One moment she lay above him, and the next second she found herself staring up at him, the bed beneath them, and him easing his way between her thighs. Throwing her head back to expose her long neck, she begged, "Do it please."

"When you are stronger."

"You make me stronger." Whenever he fed, she felt able to take on the world. Feeding had brought her back. Her powers returned. He could help her heal. "Feed."

"Are you ready to feed from me in return?"

She nodded. She knew she would have to take his blood for the bonding to complete. Though her stomach protested, it settled down again. They would have to repeat this process once a month to maintain a strong tie.

He bit his wrist. Blood trickled from the two puncture marks. "When I suck, you begin."

She grasped his arm with both hands as he eased her off the bed. He moved behind her so her back rested against his front, giving him better access to her neck as she fed from his wrist. With a sigh, his teeth pierced her neck and she gasped in pain but, as his lips touched her neck, she brought his wrist to her lips and sucked. Immediately, pain turned to desire as pleasure rocked through her. She could feel the cadence of his heart and then she heard it.

Slow down my love. His voice echoed in her mind. She eased back, but he stopped her. *Not yet. You still must feed, but you will make yourself sick if you rush it.*

She took his advice and continued to feed long after he stopped. Only when he gently pulled away from her did she stop drinking. How bright and colorful everything seemed. She'd always assumed in his world of darkness, he couldn't see the colors so rich and vibrant in the daylight, the colors she viewed were deeper and richer. She could see details she had missed.

Do not wander without me until you are used to my night.

Your night?

Yes, this is not the night you have seen before. I can hear it in your thoughts.

She hadn't actually spoken out loud. "You can hear me, then?"

"Yes." He spoke the words aloud before moving back into a private communication link only they shared. *As you can hear me. And I am serious. Do not wander at night without me. It will take time for you to grow accustomed to my world. If you are not careful, you will get too wrapped up in the beauty around you. The very details that you have never experienced before will mesmerize you, and if you do not pay attention to where you are, you can end up where you shouldn't be or, worse, in danger's path.*

She closed her eyes. *Can you hear me?*

I can. His serious face belied his laughter. How much of his emotion had she missed?

"Can we marry before we leave?"

You don't have to talk aloud.

"I know." She grimaced and closed her lids tight. *This is strange for me. Give me some time and it will come more naturally.*

You have all the time in the world. He kissed the line of her shoulder.

"So about getting married?"

Blissful happiness filled him, and her inability to maintain their private linked amused him. *Yes. I have inquired about staying on another week already. Is that enough time to plan a wedding?*

"I only have one request."

A different ring? He smirked. *It's pretty hideous. Mother insisted I couldn't propose empty-handed, but you may have your pick of the family heirlooms when we return.*

"Your mother?"

She hopes to really get to know you when we

return.

"And you? What do you hope for when we go home?"

"Spending the rest of my days making you happy and proving to the world I'm worthy of my witchy wife's love." This time the words weren't in her head but spoken aloud so the wind could carry them to all those listening. Because words spoken to the universe held a promise beyond their mended bond.

"I love you, Silvano."

"I plan to never make you doubt those words, princess."

"I believe you."

"Our first agenda when we get off the island is to move into a house of our own. A place you can call home. Perhaps, when you are ready, we can talk babies again."

Making room for him on the bed, she eased into the strength of his embrace. She never would have believed he spoke of love truthfully, if he hadn't done so of his own free will. Only in breaking their mating bond had they truly found each other. And she planned to never let him go again.

Epilogue

Everyone asked whether he planned to permanently move into Rekkus and Dana's house, and Cyrus didn't have an answer. A full week after the summoning and he only ventured from the beach on rare occasions. To check on Janessa. To give Dana some peace when she fell asleep one afternoon. He and Serena played with the babies on the beach, allowing their mama a much-needed rest. And once he had ventured back to his room. But the ghosts there seemed too much. The silence allowed him to think. He didn't want to think.

The noise of the triplets quieted his mind, and the sleepless nights kept him from dreaming. He didn't need either. He remained quiet on the beach this night. He held Brynn, who had squirmed and fussed through the moonlight wedding service for Silvano and Janessa. Sage officiated as she had for every other marriage on the island. And, although the party raged outside, Cyrus had no desire to celebrate life.

"What are you doing in here by yourself?" Dana's worried voice cut through his pity party.

"I am hardly alone. Brynn is with me."

"Brynn is never good company at this time of night." She bent to kiss his downy head.

Cyrus shrugged, keeping one hand on the baby and the other arm flung over his eyes. "He is perfect company for me."

She stood there, and he could sense her concern. He knew she gnawed her bottom lip, eyes cast down, and he knew she wanted to question him. Wanted to know what had been so bad at the summoning he hadn't spoken to any of his siblings since.

Rekkus came in with his daughter under his arm like a knapsack, squealing and giggling, her little bum shaking and legs kicking in delight as she tried to get loose. "Why?"

"You hate parties," they chorused.

"Exactly why am I the only one out there when I am usually the only one in here?"

"Why do you do anything you do, Rekkus?" Cyrus asked, suddenly angry at his friend for all he had. Everything Cyrus never would. Over the last few days, his anger at the larger man had been building.

Rekkus sniffed the air and stared at him. Cyrus refused to break eye contact. Let the tiger do it. Of course, he hadn't expected they would still be staring each other down five minutes later. The man never lost at anything. "Fuck you, Rekkus."

Dana squeaked in surprise, but Rekkus made no sound as, with slow, precise movements, he handed his daughter off to his wife...who had another baby asleep in a sling on her back. He reached down and lifted his sleeping son off his friend. Which pissed Cyrus off. How dare he remove the one thing bringing him any peace.

"Take the cubs and leave, Dana. Now." He kept his gaze fixed in the distance.

"Don't talk to her that way."

Rekkus growled, "Dana, now."

Dana froze, arms full of wide-eyed babies. "Rekkus."

"It's always your way isn't it, oh great tiger king?" Anger rushed through Cyrus. "You are always right, you know best. Well, you should have let them get me that night. I wish you had let them kill me. Anything would be better than this."

"Dana. Out. Now."

This time she didn't hesitate. She turned on her heels and ran out the door. By the time it closed behind her, he knew she headed for his siblings. Well, what did it matter? Myron's fucking cards would know what was happening, and she would tell them anyhow. No one could have a secret on this island if they tried. But he did, and it was killing him.

"Repeat that," Rekkus demanded.

A part of him wanted to defy the order, but anger and satisfaction spurred him on. "I said I wish I had died that night."

"Well, you didn't."

"Fuck you." With every ounce of anger he could pull forth, Cyrus clenched a fist and swung, connecting with Rekkus's chin. He welcomed the pain shooting up his arm and through his hand. Welcomed feeling something tangible.

"Feel better?" Rekkus demanded, his eyes glowing.

"Ready to shift?" Cyrus taunted.

Rekkus threw back his head and had the audacity to laugh. "You couldn't handle my tiger."

And Cyrus went for the one thing he could think of to hurt the man, to push his best friend away. "A little poison in your kibble seems to bring the tiger down."

Cyrus should have been prepared. He'd known it was coming, but it had been so long since Rekkus had struck him he had actually forgotten the shocking power, the immediate tremor of the hit followed by the pain. Not content, Rekkus picked him up and threw him through the shuttered window.

Adrenaline pumped through him, pushing him to his feet. Cyrus jumped back through the window, rushing Rekkus with a shoulder to the stomach. Unprepared for the move, Rekkus stumbled into the coffee table, taking both of them to the floor, the table smashing into pieces under them. Rekkus kicked Cyrus off him, sending him into the sofa which in turn broke apart under the assault.

Scrambling to his feet, Cyrus grabbed a chair and placed it between them. Rekkus paused, "Are you shitting me? A chair?"

"Well, if you had a whip, I would use it, too."

Rekkus's openmouthed glare broke the tension. Cyrus burst into a fit of laughter and Rekkus snorted, waving away Cyrus and his ridiculous chair. Rekkus stepped over broken glass and other debris and grabbed four beers from the fridge. He handed two to Cyrus before sitting on the floor with his back against the wall. He opened one and chugged while placing the other against his eye. "Okay, lion tamer, want to tell me what the hell is going on before everyone on this island bursts through the door?"

Cyrus sat on the chair, unsure if he could get up if he sat on the floor. He also didn't know if he wanted to drink the beer or place both on his aches and pains. "It's nothing."

"Bullshit."

"I don't want to talk about it."

"I don't care."

Cyrus swallowed. "I had four visitors at the summoning."

"Four? How the hell could you have four when only three died that night?" Rekkus put his beers down and leaned forward.

"Ah, but unbeknownst to us, there was a fourth."

"Cyrus, I found only three bodies"—he paused—"not caused by me."

It had taken weeks for the Syndicate to figure out how many Rekkus tore apart.

"Her name was Lara, and she was my soul mate." Cyrus took a chug and wiped his bloody mouth with his sleeve. Which he immediately regretted as the cuts on his lips sent pain shooting up his face. "How bad is this lip?"

"Like you injected a plum into it. Don't change the subject. Lara?"

"Apparently, someone used soul mate trackers to find mine. They ambushed her in her home at the same time they attacked my sisters. They wanted no trace left behind."

"Well, they failed."

"Thanks to you."

"Thanks or curse?"

Cyrus sighed. How he hated eating crow. "I didn't mean it, Rekkus."

"I know. You wanted me to get angry and fight you. You feel better?"

"Define better."

Dana's gasp interrupted the scene. She handed each baby off to one of the Rowan siblings standing around her. Once she could see both men were okay, she entered the room, pausing and closing her eyes when glass crunched beneath her feet. She moved into the bedroom and shut the door with such careful precision it belied her anger.

"I suggest you two run," Cemil whispered.

They didn't, of course, but all eyes remained on the closed door.

Five minutes later, Dana came out with three fully packed bags. Rekkus jumped up. "Where are you going?"

"Don't." She put up a hand, marched over to Cemil, handed him her bags, and grabbed Rhys from him. Rhys giggled and let out a roar, the same one the baby did whenever he was about to shift. "*Peidiwch â hyd yn oed yn meddwl am y peth.*"

The baby, who had never once stopped his shift for even Rekkus, looked wide-eyed at his mother; Dana had never spoken a word of Welsh in her life. Not only the baby, but the rest of the room stared at her in awe until Rhys burst into tears, snuggling into her neck.

"When did you learn to speak Welsh?" Cyrus couldn't remember Rekkus saying she was learning the other language.

Rekkus blinked at his mate. "Dana?"

Cyrus shifted his gaze to Rekkus. "You didn't know either."

"Shut up, Cyrus." Rekkus's voice held something never heard from the tiger—panic. "Dana, where are you going?"

"This is no longer a home, Rekkus. This is a

pigsty. I am going to find a place to sleep." She put up her free hand. "Not with you."

"Dana, it was my fault." Cyrus took inventory of the damage. Guilt racked him.

"Oh, I am well aware who's at fault. You have an entire island to fight on, and you choose here, my home." Dana vented her ire on Cyrus and, when Rekkus smiled, she turned on him. "And you, my mate. You could have simply picked him up and taken him somewhere else to fight. So I don't want to see either of you until my house is fixed back the way it was."

Cyrus waited until Dana left with the Rowans in tow to ask, "What did she say to the baby?"

"Don't even think about it." Rekkus rifled through the cabinets in the kitchen.

"Think about what?"

"Ah, this should do it." He slammed a bottle of whiskey on the counter and pulled out two glasses. "She said 'Don't even think about it'"

Cyrus picked up a piece of broken table before dropping it again. "Are we fixing the house or getting drunk."

"I plan to do both."

"Good plan."

Rekkus lifted his glass and shot back the amber liquid. He repeated the action twice before starting to collect the broken furniture pieces and throw them out the broken window. Despite the destruction, Cyrus didn't feel anything but numb, blissfully empty. He had been close to saying to hell with it all and jumping through the next portal. But maybe Rekkus's fist had rattled his brain back into place. Or the shock of Dana taking control, or perhaps the comical idea Cemil really thought anyone could outrun Dana's wrath. Any of those might have been enough to allow him to keep going but, in the end, Sarka cuddling with the baby had made him pause. She had surreptitiously breathed in the baby smell and kissed the curly-haired boy. And as she rocked, he saw a soft side he had long thought he would never see from her again. And he felt something he hadn't in a long time.

Hope.

He still felt guilt and had a lot to find out. He needed to learn more about Lara. Needed to know if she truly was his soul mate or had been killed by accident. Or sent to simply screw with him, but, either way, he needed to know. Until then, he had a bottle of alcohol to help empty and a cabin to fix.

He couldn't help but be pleased when he saw the telltale signs of a black eye forming on Rekkus's face. If nothing else, knowing he had landed one good punch was like earning a trophy. After all, the little things in life kept a man going.

"Are you going to stand there beaming because you landed a punch or two, or are you gonna help me clean up?"

"She's only been gone a few minutes and you are already itchy. I can't wait to see you by morning."

"You are joking."

Cyrus thought it best not to answer as he grabbed the broom. Rekkus shook his head. Perhaps a warlock grabbing a broom was a bit cliché. But it was nice to have something normal or at least their form of normal.

Through the window, he saw Kaleb and some of the security team sitting, watching with a bowl of popcorn before them. This would only end with everyone up at the training fields and someone coming in to fix up the cabin because no one wanted Rekkus back in the Haus.

In the end, everything seemed to be as it should. They were family for better or worse. And he wouldn't have it any other way.

About the Author

Award-winning author Dominique Eastwick grew up a US Navy Brat, so if there was a naval base, that was probably home. She currently resides in North Carolina with her husband, two children, crazy lab and lazy cat.

Dominique's love of reading started when she was told to read *To Kill a Mockingbird* in high school. A book that opened her eyes to the joys of reading and entering into the world of the author. To this day she ranks this book as her favorite.

Stay connected with my Newsletter:
http://eepurl.com/brjq6D

Also by Dominique Eastwick